The Rise of Promise

(The Wolves of Promise Falls, Book 2)

T. S. JOYCE

The Rise of Promise

ISBN: 9798448568886
Copyright © 2022, T. S. Joyce
First electronic publication: April 2022

T. S. Joyce
www. tsjoyce.com

NOTE FROM THE AUTHOR:

This book is a work of fiction. The names, characters, places, and incidents are products of the writer's imagination or have been used fictitiously and are not to be construed as real. Any resemblance to persons, living or dead, actual events, locale or organizations is entirely coincidental. The author does not have any control over and does not assume any responsibility for third-party websites or their content.

Published in the United States of America

First digital publication: April 2022
First print publication: April 2022

DEDICATION

For the 1010 Roundup Crew.

Let's make this year's event epic!

ACKNOWLEDGMENTS

You readers have done more for me and my stories than I can even explain on this teeny page. You found my books, and ran with them, and every share, review, and comment makes release days so incredibly special to me.

1010 is magic and so are you.

ONE

Tonight, Stark Wulfson was a hunter.

Scratch that. Stark was a hunter every night, but tonight he was stalking something very different than his usual prey in the woods. Tonight, he was hunting his ex-Alpha.

Tessa Hoda should've left town when the new Alpha, Daylen, had told her to. Yet here she was sauntering into Zaps Bar and Grill, dressed in an oversize hoodie with the hood up, looking as suspicious as a cunning she-wolf could look. She tossed a look behind her before she opened the front door of the bar, but she wouldn't recognize his truck. Why? Because he'd traded in his Camaro, his baby, for this diesel truck to haul the new home he'd just bought himself.

Tessa disappeared inside, and that was his cue.

Stark slipped out of his truck and shoved his hands deep into his pockets. It was a warm night as spring had officially sprung in Leadville, Colorado, but putting his hands in his pockets was a habit.

As he made his way around to the back door, he scented the air. If Tessa's footprints weren't clear as day in the mud around the side of the building, the smell of her perfume would've been a dead giveaway. She'd tried to get in the back way, but her problem was her social skills. You see, Tessa was hated, and justly, but Stark? He could charm the pants off a nun. It was his gift.

Plus, he knew the people who worked here. Kind of.

The back door was locked, as he expected it to be, so he rang the buzzer. It took a good forty-five seconds before the peephole-window opened. All he could see was the top of a head of brunette hair. It had stripes of blonde in it now, but he recognized the part, and the voice as she said, "Go around the front."

"Lyndi, it's me," Stark murmured.

Lyndi stood up on her tiptoes and glared at him.

Her eyes were red, and her cheeks were damp.

"Whoa," he uttered, shocked at her disheveled appearance. Lyndi was always put together. "Did you splash water on your face?"

"No. I'm crying. Go away."

"Ew." And Stark considered it—going away. He looked longingly to the parking lot where his new rig sat right at the curb, ready to book it to Main Street and back into the mountains where he belonged.

But...

"Tessa's here."

The door unlocked with an echoing click, and Lyndi pulled it open. In a rush, she ran her knuckles over her cheeks to dry them. She wouldn't meet his eyes. "Why is she still in town?"

"Hell if I know. She's been poking around all of Daylen and Denver's favorite spots, and last night she got bold enough to come into Daylen's territory. I could smell her wolf all over those woods when I woke up this morning."

"Maybe she's here for a drink," Lyndi muttered, her shoulders slumped.

"More likely she's here to fuck with you."

"Why me?"

5

"Because you're Denver's sister, and it's a way to get to Daylen." Stark narrowed his eyes. "Without telling me all your girl-shit, which I don't care about at all, what's wrong with your leaking eyeballs?"

"Oh, you know. Just falling apart." She threw her arms into the air and led the way down the hallway to a storage room. "Everything's on fire, but I'll survive. I'm very tough."

"Great. Well, if you need anything, don't ask me. I don't do emotions." He gave her a little salute and stalked toward the bar area to see what Tessa was up to.

"Stark?"

"No," he said over his shoulder.

"If you see Denver tonight, could you have her call me back?"

Stark frowned and stopped in his tracks, then turned slowly. "She isn't answering you?"

Tears streamed down Lyndi's cheeks and her face crumpled as she slumped back against the wall. "I really need her tonight, but I think she's out with Daylen." She lifted her gaze to him, and her eyes were blazing the gold of her fox. He hadn't seen this much heartbreak on a face in a while.

"You need to put on sunglasses," he muttered, gesturing to her face.

She just stared at him like she hadn't heard a word he'd said.

Stark shoved his hands in his pockets again, and cast a glance toward the bar before looking back to Lyndi. "Look, maybe you should leave work early—"

"I'm not working tonight."

"Oh. Then why are you here?"

"Because I didn't want to be alone."

"Fuck a bucket," he growled as he canted his head. "Lyndi, get your ass to that bathroom and clean up your fuckin' face—"

"You're being rude—"

"You need rude. You can't fall apart." He closed the distance between them and gripped her arms, leveled her with his gaze. "You're Lyndi motherfucking Mosley. Say it."

"What?"

"Repeat it. I'm Lyndi motherfucking Mosley."

"I'm Lyndi mother…"

"…fucking Mosley, and I'm a badass. I'm a fox shifter. I could eat any one of those pitiful little humans in the next room. I'm Goliath! Repeat it!"

"I'm badass, and a fox shifter, and I eat people."

"Oh God, that's good enough. Look, you're hot. Too hot to be crying like this. And what have you done to your hair?" he demanded, lifting a streak of the platinum blond between his fingers.

"I was spiraling and I thought highlights would make me feel better, but now I look like a skunk!" She was on the verge of wailing.

"A hot skunk. Repeat it!"

"I'm…" she frowned and swallowed hard, sniffed, then said, "I'm a hot skunk."

"Now go wipe those tears off your face, get your life together, and come back out to the bar. I will have one of those god-awful blended mango margaritas waiting for you, because there isn't a thing in the world a margarita can't fix. For girls. A margarita would make me yak, and probably suck my dick up into me and create a vag—"

"How do you know what kind of drinks I drink?" Her pert little nose was all wrinkled up, her lashes had water on them, her eyes were the bright hue of molten gold, and her cheeks were all pink. She really was a pretty little skunk…errr…fox.

Honesty was best. "I pay attention to everything. I

have to. It's how I was built."

There was a question in her eyes, but before she could ask him something he wasn't ready to answer, he played defense and asked her a question instead. "Why aren't you afraid of Tessa? I told you she's here, and you don't even smell scared. Why not?"

Lyndi shrugged up her shoulders and told him, "I'm not afraid of anything anymore."

And then she turned and made her way to the bathroom, leaving Stark to wonder what the hell had happened to the little fox to kill her fear of the wolf.

Stark pulled his phone out of his back pocket and opened a text to his Alpha's mate, Denver.

Come get your sister, she's at Zaps dancing on a bar top. Send.

There. His duty was done. He wasn't a babysitter for some broken-hearted, bleeding-heart, emotionally-charged woman. Didn't matter how pretty she was.

He would rather stick his pecker in a fire ant mound than ever see tears again.

TWO

Her hair really did look like a skunk pelt.

Lyndi slathered on another layer of foundation to cover the red in her cheeks, and blinked several times, like that would get rid of puffiness. She looked like hot garbage in a dumpster that was rolling down a hill on fire.

No wonder Jake had become so uninterested in improving himself for her.

A snarl rattled up her throat, and she swallowed it down as the bathroom door opened. A twenty-something blonde smiled at her and disappeared into a stall. It was Friday night, and she actually had the day off for mental health reasons, per Gary the Bartender, and yet here she was.

Why? Because her job was literally the only thing that made sense in her life right now, and she needed an anchor to keep her from floating up into space and losing her way completely.

Maybe her hair would look better in a ponytail. Nope. A messy bun hid the bad dye job a little better. She would worry about fixing it tomorrow, before her tattoo appointment and getting her nails painted glossy black.

She'd never spiraled quite like this before.

The desperation to change herself into someone entirely different for a little while was overwhelming. She just wanted to escape the discomfort of her own skin.

Stark had seen her in the worst moment of her life. Stark, of all people.

He was the most careless, most dangerous, most aggressively annoying, most unstable, most antagonizing, most obnoxiously hot werewolf in existence. Now, she'd never met all the werewolves in existence, but she felt pretty safe in feeling like he was the gnarliest.

Her mortification would be infinite tomorrow, when she felt anything but the thousand-pound glugging broken heart in her chest cavity.

One more layer of mascara, and she put her emergency makeup kit back into her purse.

Boobs out, chin up. Your life isn't over. It's just going to look very different from today on.

Jake had really done it.

She was the biggest failure in the fox shifter community, and by tomorrow night, everyone would know it.

Maybe she should become a hermit and live in the mountains in a hidden shack, raise baby goats, throw her cell phone into Promise Falls, and lose all contact with society.

Starting tomorrow, she was determined to do just that, but for tonight? She was going to do her best to take a breath and absorb the happy chatter around her.

She shouldered her purse and pushed open the heavy, swinging bathroom door, then tromped down the hallway, forcing her chin up higher.

As Stark had promised, there was a mango margarita sitting on the bar top, but someone had placed a rubber film over it. She sat down on the stool right in front of it and cocked her head. Was that a...?

"Who put a condom on my drink?" she asked Gary the Bartender. His real name wasn't Gary, but Denver had called him that so many times, the name had stuck in Lyndi's head.

Gary was behind the bar pouring a line of shots with a deep frown on his dark features. He twitched his head toward the back corner, where Stark sat next to Tessa Hoda, embroiled in some deep conversation that had both of them looking pissed.

Gary told her, "That guy put one on your drink and told me it was so I don't drug you. I tried to explain I'm the one who made the drink and that I'm friends with you, and you are my boss, and I'm not the type to drug girls, but he growled like an animal and called me a 'waffle' and walked away, and that's the story of how your margarita got a magnum condom over the top of it." Gary scoffed. "Magnum."

She popped the rubber ring off the lip of the glass and put it on top of the packaging trash he'd left behind.

"He probably left that trash there so you could see the size of the condom. Magnum," Gary scoffed again.

"He probably didn't," she uttered, reaching for a

straw. "More likely he's just messy."

"You know that guy?"

"Yep." She took a long drag of the margarita and let it fill her mouth. "There's no alcohol in this, is there?" she asked suspiciously. It tasted too good.

"Nope. He ordered you a non-alcoholic one. Said something about 'skunks don't spiral well.'"

Lyndi snorted a laugh. Okay, that had caught her off guard.

She took another sip and twisted back around to study Stark's profile. He looked different than he had when he lived here before. He'd only recently moved back to Leadville after two years of being away on some mystery mission with the rest of his wolf Pack, but that time away had done him good. He used to have shaggy blond hair that covered most of his face, but now he had shaved the sides and wore the mohawk in a topknot that accentuated his chiseled cheekbones and bright-blue eyes. He wore a burgundy T-shirt over black work pants, and boots that looked well-worn. The strong curves of his shoulders stretched the thin material of his shirt, and dayum. Maybe the Lost Wolf, as the entire shifter community called him, had been working out more.

His lips were twisted into a snarl with whatever Tessa was saying to him. He cast Lyndi a quick glance, like he knew she was ogling him. She felt busted thinking about how hot he was, so she looked away as fast as she could. That flash of blue in his eyes had been so bright. He must've been very angry at Tessa.

The sound of Tessa's chair scooting backward hard rang against Lyndi's oversensitive ears, and her shoes thudded against the floor as she strode closer and closer. *Don't react*, her inner fox said softly. The animal had been quiet since she'd heard what Jake` was about to do to her.

She could smell the wolf and the fur and the dominance, and it grew overpowering as Tessa settled on the stool next to her. "Lucky little fox," she purred. "You got yourself a little guard dog tonight."

Lyndi slid a glare to the ex-Alpha of the Sheridan Pack. "Look, I've had a real shitty day. I don't have enough patience left in my body for one of your fuckin' riddles, Tessa. What do you want?"

"For you to give Denver and Daylen a little message for me."

Shhhhit. "And what is that?" Oh, she already knew the answer. She could see it in that evil she-wolf's sharp-toothed grin.

Tessa flinched back with a closed fist, and okay. The humans were in for a show tonight. Tessa was fast, but Lyndi's fox reflexes were something else, and she was fueled by being a woman scorned and then targeted for no good reason.

She lurched out of the way of Tessa's incoming fist and blasted a punch across the woman's face so hard that Tessa went flying off the bar stool, and Lyndi went off balance too.

Her chair clattered to the floor as Tessa stood.

Gary's yelling and Stark's booming laugh covered the growl that rattled from Tessa as she stood slowly, facing off with Lyndi.

"You should remember your place," Tessa growled.

"Pretty sure she just showed you her place," Stark said, hands on his knees as he huffed laughter. "Oh God. I'm crying. Am I crying?" He wiped his fingers under his dancing eyes. "I've never cried before. That was awesome. Is your nose broken?"

Tessa's eyes blazed gold, and she bunched her muscles to jump at Lyndi. In that second, everything changed. The clatter of yelling bar patrons morphed to a roaring sound in her ears, and she braced to take Tessa's impact. Time slowed for a single moment, and she could see it all so clearly. Tessa reaching for her.

Stark's smile had faded, and he placed himself in front of Lyndi. Tessa's hand stretched out, and her nails clawed across Lyndi's cheek as Stark absorbed the impact with such force, the floors shook and the front windows shattered. Their collision was like a bomb going off.

Lyndi flinched, but when she opened her eyes again, Stark and Tessa were gone.

Just...gone.

All that remained were the townies hunkered down with matching looks of baffled confusion as they looked around.

Gary whispered, "What the fuck?"

The front door swung closed, and Lyndi bolted for the back exit.

Stark wouldn't fight Tessa in the front parking lot where people could see. Probably. He was smarter than that. Also probably.

He would take her somewhere out of sight, and there were woods behind Zaps.

Lyndi hopped over the stairs and sprinted for the

tree line. Tessa was an ex-Alpha and horrifically dominant. If Stark was in trouble, it had something to do with Lyndi, and she couldn't leave him to Tessa's teeth without backup.

Wait. What? What was she doing?

Lyndi forced her legs to stop.

Why are we stopping? The fox screamed in her head.

Drip, drip, drip.

The scent of blood filled the air. Her blood. Lyndi brushed her fingertips against her burning cheek. Tessa had clawed her deeper than she'd thought. Skank.

And then she heard it—the snarling in the woods.

She'd been right. Stark had dragged the fight out here. Lyndi should leave. This was werewolf business and she was just a fox. She'd lost her mind in there and engaged with Tessa, and thinking about that now, it hit her how badly that could've ended up.

Her head was foggy from the Jake stuff and she wasn't thinking straight.

She tried to back up toward the bar, but her fox was being stubborn. Why? She'd never even paid attention to Stark before, and now she wanted to go involve herself in a wolf fight? A motherfreaking werewolf fight?

Clearly, her fox was suicidal.

The snarling was getting louder, more volatile. Without her telling her legs to go, she drifted in the direction of the sound.

She felt like she was in a dream as she stepped over roots and under low-hanging pine branches. Faster and faster she hiked, until at last, she saw them.

The wolves were a blur of violence like none she'd ever witnessed before.

The wolves had two different tones to their fur— one light gray, one dark. She had never seen Stark or Tessa Changed, so had no idea which was which.

Slowly, she crouched down, overwhelmed by the sound of war and her own heartbeat roaring in her head.

The scent of blood was stronger here, and as the wolves disengaged and slowly circled each other, she could see their fur matted with dark, wet spots. They were shredding each other.

The light gray one looked right at her, and Lyndi froze. Tessa's blazing-gold eyes bore straight through her soul, and now she could tell them apart.

The dark gray wolf positioned himself in front of Lyndi. He flattened his ears back, tossed her a frosty-blue glare, and curled his lips back to expose blood-soaked, razor-sharp teeth. *Go.*

And her fox listened.

Just like that, she stood and backed away. Lyndi couldn't stop if she tried.

What the hell? The fox had wanted to help him and now she was abandoning him? This made no sense to her. No sense at all!

Lyndi tried to stop herself, but she couldn't. Instead, the fox pushed her body to turn and run back toward the lights she could barely see shining through the trees.

Zaps will be safe, the animal assured her. *Stark will stop her.*

"Okay, psycho," she whispered out loud. "You don't even know Stark."

No, you don't know Stark. He can kill Tessa. He will if we stay. He doesn't want to.

The ringing of her phone in her back pocket interrupted the jumble of confused thoughts rattling around her head. One look at the screen and she huffed a relieved sigh and accepted Denver's call.

"Where's Stark?" Denver demanded.

Over the phone, Lyndi could hear the roar of a truck engine and Denver's mate, Daylen, talking to her in the background. "Ask her if they're still at Zaps. He's fighting now."

"He is!" Lyndi said, running past the final row of trees and into the small clearing behind the bar. Some of the people from inside were talking in groups outside. "He's in the woods out back. It's Tessa."

"We know. Daylen can hear them through his bond to Stark. Stark just blew it wide open. Daylen can't even fucking see where we are. He just sees woods and Tessa. I'm driving. We will be there in two minutes. Do not follow them out there!"

"Okay, I'm going to keep the humans from the woods," Lyndi huffed out.

She disconnected the call and shoved her phone back into her pocket and then held her hands out to calm Gary, who was jogging toward her.

"Oh my God, Lyndi, I thought something happened to you. Why the hell did you run out like that?"

"Everything is okay—"

"Whoa! What's wrong with your eyes?" Gary hunched down and his hands hovered right over her skin, like he wanted to cup her cheeks.

"What? Nothing!" Shoot, her eyes were probably bright gold and she had exactly zero pairs of sunglasses on her. She swatted his hands away. "Focus. That was so weird in there. The windows are broken. Do you know how much that is going to cost us to replace?"

"You're bleeding," Gary said, and every emotion on his face said he had red flags blaring all through his head. "You're bleeding and your eyes are straight gold, and you were in the woods, and what the fuck is going on, Lyndi?"

"I don't know," she lied, careful to keep her eyes angled anywhere but at him.

"I already called the police," he told her, backing away a few steps. His frown looked mighty suspicious.

Dammit. "Uh, why?"

"Uuuuh, because that woman clawed your face, and they broke the windows and disappeared like fuckin' aliens."

"Right. Okay, good." She could already hear the

sirens as she texted Denver. *Take Danner Street and cut through the woods that way. Police at Zaps.* Send.

"Come on, Gary, I need you to go calm the customers down. I don't want this weird stuff to scare them off of the bar."

"My name isn't Gary! And the police are going to want to talk to you. Where are you going?" he called from behind her, where he definitely wasn't following.

"I'm bleeding, remember?" she clipped out simply as she motored toward the back entrance of the bar. He didn't need to know that she would heal these claw marks in a few hours, tops. Mostly, she needed to take a minute to control her inner fox before she talked to anyone else of the human variety.

Today was the worst, weirdest, most surprising day of her life.

Stark wasn't at all like she'd thought.

He was out in those woods fighting the devil herself because of Lyndi. She knew he was. He was protecting her, but why?

Stark had never had a nice thing to say to her before today.

THREE

You can't watch over her forever.

Tessa's words echoed through Stark's throbbing head.

He lifted his phone up to connect a call to his boss, but caught his reflection on the screen. He looked like roadkill. His face was seven shades of blue and all cut to hell, and his shoulders and torso were worse.

A text came through from his Alpha. Daylen said, *Come home. Denver made you breakfast.*

At the bar getting Bloody Marys. Send. He loved texting because he could lie all he wanted.

No you aren't. You're watching Lyndi. She's okay. Marsden is tracking Tessa and she's still three states away. Come home.

Another thing he loved about texting—his Alpha's orders didn't work on his wolf, because he couldn't hear the command in Daylen's voice via text. Ka-ching.

Stark connected a call to Gerald, his boss at the roof construction site.

"Please tell me you aren't calling in sick today," Gerald answered.

"Of course not. I'm calling in sick for the next three days."

"Stark! What did we talk about last week?"

"Ummmm, you said I do the work of three crew members—"

"—when you work—"

"—and that I'll probably get employee of the month—"

"—that you'll never get employee of the month if you don't listen to instructions—"

"—and then we talked about how your instructions are dumb and everything takes twice as long, and then I made a list of ways to be more efficient and you implemented my ideas. I guess we're doing all right because we are three to five days ahead of schedule on this project. I'm asking for three days off, Gerald. You don't have to pay me. I'll come back and be me again, doing the work of three men for the pay of one."

"I want a reason you need the time off, and you better not give me some lame, half-assed excuse."

Stark inhaled deeply and gave himself three seconds to try and gather his patience. He didn't like answering to humans. He stared at Lyndi's front door, with its coat of mustard-yellow paint and decorative wreath, and decided to throw his boss a bone.

"There's a girl. She needs protecting for a few days, and for whatever godforsaken reason, I've decided I'm the man for the job."

Gerald was silent for several moments, and then quietly said, "All right. See you Thursday morning."

The line went dead and Stark gritted his teeth and shook his head in annoyance. He should've just killed Tessa and gotten it over with—taken the mark on his soul, used his last chance, let Daylen put him down like he was sanctioned to do if Stark killed any more wolves.

Lost Wolf. That's the name he'd earned, and that's the name he deserved. Since age fourteen, he'd burned his way through countless Packs, fighting anyone who looked at him wrong, and winning way too easily, way too many times.

This really was his last chance Pack.

The door of Lyndi's townhome opened, and the scent of fox and perfume hit his nose. He sniffed just to get a second whiff. She smelled good when she was all riled up and her animal was on the surface. He bet her fox was pretty. All red and black and golden-eyed. She probably had a good little bite to her, too. He'd been shocked to his bones when she'd popped Tessa on Friday night. It was a stupid move, because Tessa would kill her now, but it was funny at the time. And impressive.

She had as much fire as Denver. Maybe more.

She was wearing a red floral sundress that hit at the knees, a jean jacket, and brown leather boots. Sometime since Friday night, she'd adjusted her highlights from bright blonde to a caramel color in her nearly-black hair. She'd straightened her tresses and they hung around her shoulders, lifting gently in the early spring breeze as she fumbled with her keys to lock her door. She was carrying a black tote bag, and also a clipboard, binder, and folder, and her purse on the other shoulder.

Three curse words drifted to him on the wind when she dropped her folder and scattered the papers on the welcome mat. The hem of her red dress blew skyward and she yelped as she dropped her purse to try and tame the flyaway clothes.

Black lace panties? Hell. Yes.

Stark adjusted his hardening dick and rolled down the window. A gentleman would offer to help her. "Nice ass."

"Aaaah!" Lyndi yelled, spinning fast enough to drop the binder too. "Stark?" she asked, still at war with her dress. Her eyes were the straight gold of her animal. Her makeup was all done up—dark around the eyes with a pretty shade of pink shiny shit on her lips. Her cheeks matched. The claw marks from the fight with Tessa had healed completely.

"Where are you going?"

"Ummmm…" She looked around like she was searching for inspiration. "Just…out."

"Cool, I'll give you a ride."

"Look, I'm running late already—"

"Good thing I know how to drive fast. Hop in."

"No thanks. I need to do this alone."

Stark narrowed his eyes at her. "Do what alone?" Maybe she had a date. He didn't like that. He also didn't like how much that thought bothered him.

Lyndi ignored him, so he got out and jogged over to her, helped her scoop up her things, and read the top of one of the papers.

It was a typed-out letter. "Dear council, I'm requesting time to work out the pairing with Jake Smallwell, and pleading that you reconsider—"

Lyndi ripped the paper out of his hand and shoved it into the folder. "Go away, Stark."

"What's going on? Why would the council be involved in your pairing? And most importantly, why the hell would you want to prolong anything with that dork? He probably wears socks when you fuck—ow!"

Lyndi had shoved him right on one of his injuries from the fight with Tessa the other night. He was healing, but not fast enough for his liking.

She bustled past him, but dropped her keys in the yard when she was almost to her car. "Crap on a cracker!" she yelled.

"It's probably God telling you to get in my truck," he reasoned.

"God would never tell any woman to do anything with you."

"I'll make you a deal."

"I don't have time for deals," she said as she stooped for the keys.

"You're about to go do something hard, right?"

Squatted down in the yard, Lyndi looked up at him, and her eyes churned with something deep he didn't understand. Something that scared him a little, because for the first time in his life, he wanted to fix something for a stranger. That was a dangerous game for his wolf.

"Yes," she said, her voice breaking on the word.

"Are your parents going to be there?"

She shook her head.

"Denver?" he asked.

Another shake of the head. "I told you, I have to do this alone."

And he considered leaving her to her little secrets. He really did. Stark looked at his truck and considered saying "fuck it" and heading to work instead of digging deeper into the mystery that was Lyndi Mosley. The problem was his damn wolf wouldn't allow it.

"You shouldn't do hard things alone," he murmured. Approaching slow, he offered his hand and helped her up. "Let's go do your mystery errand and then I'll buy you the cheapest steak in town." He offered the charming smile he'd mastered that usually worked on women.

"Since when do you care, Stark?"

He shrugged. If he answered, "I don't," she would hear the lie in his voice, so instead, he told her, "Maybe I'm just trying to get in your pants." When he said shocking things, shifters didn't really look for truths and lies. They just got disappointed looks on their faces, like Lyndi had right now.

"Nice try. I hate all men, and will until the day I croak."

"The anger will pass," he said as he took the bag, disheveled folder, and binder from her.

"How do you know?"

"Because A, you're trying to get back with an ex who is a total dweeb and not even good enough for you, and number two, you like dick, Lyndi Mosley." He sauntered toward his truck and said loud enough for her to hear, "Do you know where you find dicks? On men. We are good for some things."

She wasn't following, but that was okay. Sometimes stubborn women needed time so they would think ideas were theirs. Lyndi was one of those stubborn women, thank God. It made her much more fun than the submissive ones who went along with anything he said. He liked spirit in a woman. Sass was sexy.

He loaded her stuff into the back seat, then shut the door and leaned on his truck. He crossed his arms and canted his head. "We're running late."

Lyndi sighed and narrowed her pretty, blazing-gold eyes at him. "I have rules," she clipped out as she stomped toward the passenger's side of the truck.

"I'm bad at minding rules," he enlightened her as he slid in behind the wheel and shut his door.

"That's shocking. I'm shocked to my bones," she deadpanned.

It made him smile, because again, he liked sass. Stark turned the truck on and peeled out, leaving a trail of tire-smoke behind them. "Name your rules."

"Stark!" she griped, looking out the back window with her full lips parted in disapproval. "You left black tire marks on the street!"

"Good. Now every time you leave your house,

you'll think of me."

"In annoyance."

"It's still thinking of me," he pointed out. "Name the rules. Come on."

"One, you can't tell anyone about today. Not a soul. Not Denver, or Daylen, or Marsden, or some trashy skank you bring back to your tent in the woods, or—"

"Fifth wheel."

"What?"

"I upgraded my tent to a fifth wheel. It has a king size bed. You know, for all the trashy skanks I bring home." He tossed her a grin.

"Oh. Well...that's good news for you. I guess congratulations, even though I'm assuming you're still squatting on Daylen's land."

"Co-inhabitating."

"I don't think that's a word. Rule number two—"

Stark snorted and murmured, "Number two."

"Poop jokes? Really?"

"Where am I going?"

"Oh. Um, the meeting is at the Bull Room off Willow Creek Road."

"Whooo, fancy." It was the nicest place with

conference rooms in this small town.

"Rule number two," she tried again, "is that you have to stay in the truck. I'm fine with a steak dinner afterward. Good lord, I'm going to need a breather after this stupid meeting, but while I'm in there, no matter what, you have to let me do that part by myself."

Stark pursed his lips.

"Pinky promise me, Stark. I can't have any interference. I have a specific plan in mind and I can't get distracted."

"So, you're saying I'm distracting?"

"That's what you took away from that? Really?"

"You're way too pretty to be this grumpy."

"I don't even know what that means." Lyndi turned up the radio dial, hunkered down in her seat, and stared out the window at the passing trees. After a couple minutes of being quiet, she turned the radio down and asked, "Do you just say those things?"

"What things?"

"That girls are pretty? Are you just hardwired to compliment women and keep them unbalanced and uncertain and flattered and confused around you?"

That took Stark aback. He even checked her face

to make sure she was being serious, but her eyes stayed locked on him, void of a smile.

"Honestly, I've never thought about it, so I think I have to consider it before I answer." It was his cunning way of getting out of answering. She would forget the question soon and he would be in the clear. He really didn't like when people got too close to figuring any part of him out.

She swallowed hard. "I'm not usually grumpy like this. It's just a bad day." And then she changed the subject. "How was the fight the other night?"

"Awesome. I aspire to fight ex-Alphas with ego problems every chance I get. Bleeding is fun. Yay scars." His second language was sarcasm.

Lyndi cast him a studying glance, and then stared out the window again. "Thank you." She'd said it so softly, for a moment he thought he'd imagined it.

"For what?" he asked.

"Whatever is wrong with Tessa, you took the heat off me. It's been a while since someone stuck up for me."

He didn't like that at all. She was paired up. Wrong or right, her mate should've been sticking up for her. That's what mates were supposed to do. If they couldn't handle that, what was their fuckin' purpose?

Stark wanted to say that, but they'd pulled into the parking lot, and anxiety was wafting from Lyndi as she shuffled her folder, binder, and papers chaotically. "Everything will be fine."

"Yep."

She gave him a slightly psychotic smile. "My fate isn't to be alone forever, Stark. I did everything right, everything that was asked of me. I trusted the process and it won't let me down. It can't. I've been a good member of the community. This is just a bump in the road and someday, I'll be at home laughing about this. With…Jake." She scrunched up her face in disgust, but she erased it in an instant. "This is all good stuff. Fighting for this pairing is what is right."

"Or…drop Numbnuts and go live your life however you want. Fuck the community. Become a black sheep and have more fun."

"You're not helping."

"That's only because you aren't in a place to listen to sound advice yet."

Lyndi opened her mouth to argue, but nothing came out. She clamped her teeth closed and frowned.

"I'm going in. Wish me luck."

"Divorce his ass and take all his money, and then go buy yourself a few Snickers bars because you and I both know that lazy marmot doesn't have more than twenty-seven dollars in his bank account."

"Not helping," she growled at him and then slid out of the truck. It was pretty high up, and he hadn't installed side rails because it looked cooler without them. Right about now he thanked the powers-that-be for his vanity, because as Lyndi slid out of his rig, her full boobs smashed against the seat. He hadn't meant to be a perv, but it had happened so quickly he couldn't drag his gaze away fast enough.

Lyndi was a sexy vixen.

She made to shut the door, but hesitated. "Stark?"

"Yup?"

"Thanks for coming with me."

"Chin up in there, Mosley. Go get what you want. Steak afterward. I might even throw in a margarita with actual alcohol in it this time."

She huffed a laugh. It was a little one, and nervous-sounding, but it counted. That little noise in her throat settled something inside of him that he hadn't realized had coiled up tight, like a snake that had been threatened.

She got her things out of the back seat, and then he watched her stride up to the front entrance and take a seat on the bench beside the door. She checked the time on her phone, which made him want to check the time in the truck. 8:55. The meeting must've been set for 9:00 this morning.

He turned the radio dial, searching for a country station. He'd flipped through fourteen stations of straight static by the time the navy-blue Expedition pulled up and parked on the opposite side of the parking lot as him.

Jake got out of the back seat, dressed in a business suit. His blond hair had been moussed into a perfect blob on his head, and he wore sunglasses that probably cost more than Lyndi made in tips at the bar in a week. There was no way in hell Jake had bought them for himself. He bounced jobs. Not that Stark had particularly cared about the goings-on of a perfect stranger, but Denver talked about him to Daylen a lot. And Stark listened to every complaint she had about her sister's mate.

Stark was a watcher. Always had been, always would be.

And right now, he watched Jake's parents step out of the car. Or he assumed they were Jake's parents. They'd apparently matched their clothes to look like some kind of united front. Lame. Another man stepped out, and he had lawyer written all over him. Even his briefcase looked expensive.

Stark dragged his gaze to Lyndi—she looked utterly shaken. Her mouth had fallen open and her eyes were full of shock. Never in his life had he seen someone look so betrayed.

A snarl ripped from his chest. She hadn't expected this. He could see it written all over her face.

An older man stuck his head out the door and said something to Lyndi, and she nodded and stood on shaky legs.

Jake and his little band of morons brushed past her without a word, like she didn't exist, and she dropped her gaze to the ground before she looked up at Stark. And that was it. That was all he needed. That was her code word. Or not. He didn't give a shit. She'd made a rule for him to stay in the truck, but he'd been honest with her—he wasn't good at minding rules.

Stark shoved open his door, then slammed it and strode directly to her.

"He brought his family," she whispered. "That was my family, too. They fought for us to be paired up, even negotiated with my parents. And he has representation! It was just supposed to be us and three council members." Panic tainted every word that escaped her throat.

Stark gripped her shoulders. "Hey, shhhhh. You aren't alone." He arched his eyebrows and lowered his face to her level. "Whatever happens in there, you don't show them you're stung, do you understand? You hold your head up high. If I see you drop that chin for even a second, I'm making the biggest fuckin' scene you've ever seen. Losers don't win," he growled. "You're Lyndi motherfucking Mosley today, and when you wake up in the morning, no matter what, you will still be Lyndi motherfucking Mosley."

"My last name is Smallwell," she whispered.

"Ew. You took that dork's last name? Tell him he can have it back. And tell him to stop shopping for sunglasses in the women's section while you're at it."

Lyndi pursed her lips, but he saw the smile that was hiding there.

"Who are you?" he gritted out and held open the door for her.

"I'm Lyndi motherfucking Mosley," she whispered under her breath as she passed.

"Atta girl."

FOUR

Stark was definitely breaking the rules.

And not just her rules, but the rules of her people. Only fox shifters were allowed to know about fox-shifter business.

She recognized two of the council members who were sitting behind the long table near the back wall of the meeting room. Daniel Hammile and Igor Constant had both signed off on her and Jake's pairing on the day they'd committed to each other, but she'd never seen the third man before.

Jake was, of course, already kissing his ass, along with his family...who used to be her second family.

Don't cry, don't cry, don't cry. You don't know what they want yet.

Maybe they were here for good reasons. They loved her. They'd supported her and Jake, and every holiday and happy occasion for the last five years had been spent at their house. Everything was fine. Juuuust fine.

Stark had really just walked right in and closed the door behind them all, then taken a seat at one of the tables set up in front of the council. He leaned on his elbows, and with his head cocked, he watched Jake talk to the council members. His face was healing fast from his fight the other night, but he was still cut and bruised, and his right eye was swollen and blackened. Claw marks stretched out of the neck of his black T-shirt and up his throat to his jawline, and his eyes were a frosty blue right now. His teeth were clenched, making his jawline even more chiseled, and his hands were clasped in front of him. His muscular chest and shoulders pushed right up against that thin fabric of his T-shirt, and why the hell did he feel like he was eight hundred pounds of raw power filling up the entire room right now? He was making the air hard to breathe.

Currently, Jake was telling a joke about how the last time he'd seen Igor and Daniel, at least there had been an open bar. They chuckled. Great. Their mating ceremony was now the butt of a joke. Stark made a clicking sound behind his teeth. Later, this would be a funny story to tell around the campfire to Denver— Stark muscling his way into the most intimate and embarrassing meeting of Lyndi's life. Right about now, however, he was probably definitely about to make this meeting way worse.

Jake's parents and his representative took their turns talking to the council members, and all seemed to be in professional, but chipper, moods.

Lyndi stood there awkwardly. This was taking a long time. Should she bring Stark up with her? Or just leave him at the table? Maybe they wouldn't even notice him.

The stranger council member dragged his attention from Jake's mother, and the smile faded from his face when he locked eyes with Stark. "Please have a seat," he murmured to Jake and his family.

Lyndi smiled and moved toward him, her hand offered for a shake.

"Greetings won't be necessary, Ms. Mosley. Please have a seat."

She froze. Wait, what? She was being dismissed

after they'd all laughed and greeted Jake and his family? "I prefer you call me Mrs. Smallwell, as that's my name," she said softly.

"Not after today," the man said as he shuffled papers around, then adjusted the glasses on his nose.

Jake snorted and smirked at Lyndi as he took his seat next to his family.

The screeching of chair legs against the wooden floors assaulted her ears, and she twisted around to see Stark slowly pulling a chair out for her. "Best you take a seat before I rip that one's throat out." Stark's smile was empty, and his eyes had lightened a shade.

The stranger councilman leaned forward. "And who are—"

"Who are you?" Stark demanded in a tone that echoed straight through her blood and bones and awakened her mourning fox. Stark stood and locked his arms on the table. "You took the time to greet ol' Jakey the Snakey over there, but you can't give a moment introduce yourself to Lyndi? Clearly she doesn't know you, or she wouldn't have offered her hand. Say your name."

Holy. Shiitake mushrooms. No one in the universe was allowed to speak to the council like this. The room was dead silent, and heavy with Stark's simmering rage and unquestionable dominance.

"You aren't a fox."

Another empty smile from Stark. "I eat foxes for breakfast. Since Jake Smalldick brought representation, I am Lyndi Mosley's representation. Her sister has been named Second in the Promise Falls Pack, and thus Lyndi is under the protection of the local Pack." He lifted his blond brows. "Your name. And then we can get on with this meeting."

Chills rippled up Lyndi's arms at the steady venom in his tone. Stark was a jokester, but he had a whole other side to him. It was kind of hot.

Stranger Councilman looked furious. Red crept into his cheeks as he looked at Igor and Daniel, but they were looking somewhere in the general vicinity of the ground in front of Stark's table. And Lyndi couldn't blame them. She was having a hard time dragging her eyes up from the carpet too. Stark was very, very heavy when he wanted to be.

"I'm Abner Stackton, lead council member of the entire fox nation. Are you one of the men she's accused with?"

None of those words made sense to Lyndi. She sat

slowly into the chair next to Stark, and asked, "What do you mean by that?"

"We have notes and filings and proof on Jake's behalf that you have disrespected this pairing on multiple occasions and in an unforgivable fashion."

Stark looked to her, and in horror, she whispered, "There's no other men."

"What do you want?" Stark asked Jake directly.

Jake parted his lips, frowned, and then looked at the council members.

"I'm talking to you. What do you want? Why are we here?"

"I want our pairing dissolved so that I can be added back to the pool and find a suitable mate."

"Explain the rules to me—"

"We don't explain the rules to anyone who isn't a fox—"

Stark held up his hand. "I'm trying really hard not to kill all of you for this goddamn waste-of-time meeting." He lifted blazing-blue eyes up to Abner. "Explain."

Abner narrowed his eyes and a soft snarl rattled his chest. "If the pairing is dissolved, it is a huge shame on the both of them. Foxes mate for life. They don't pair up again if their mating fails."

"And if they do pair up?" Stark asked.

"Any offspring we have with unapproved partners won't be recognized by our community," Lyndi whispered. "They will be labeled outcasts. They will be shunned."

Stark nodded, and scratched his chin. "I see. What's the loophole?"

"I'm sorry?" Abner asked.

Stark leaned forward and spoke slowly. "What. Is. The loophole. What picture is Jake trying to paint so that he can pair up again?"

Abner's eyes morphed to the gold of his fox. "If a pairing is disrespected by one of the partners, and it is a big enough offense, it is deemed the fault of one, and the other is given a chance to re-join our breeding program."

Stark smiled, but his teeth were sharp and it looked like the grin of a great white shark. "Now we're getting somewhere." He flicked his fingers at Jake. "Let's have it. Tell us all the dirty deeds Lyndi has done."

"Stark," Lyndi whispered, her cheeks on fire. She didn't want to do this anymore. She wanted to leave.

"This isn't how it's supposed to work," Jake's representative said.

Stark deepened the bass in his voice, "She's cheated, right? You have all this proof? We want to see the proof. You could ask her yourself, Abner Stackton, 1411 Willoby Way, Kansas City, Kansas. You could ask her and hear the truth in her voice, just like I did."

"How...how do you know my address?" Abner asked, his eyes wide.

"I make it a point to know a lot about a lot. I need a good laugh, Abner Stackton. Show me the proof."

Jake shifted uncomfortably in his seat, and then twitched his head toward Stark. His representative clacked a small stack of papers onto the table to align them, and then took one set to the council members, and one set to Lyndi. He hesitated at the corner of their table, set the paperwork on the edge, then made his way back to his seat.

...he will never know...

...you appreciate me more than he ever could...

...I don't know if I can stay with him...

...I only think of you when I touch myself...

With a gasp, she shoved the papers away. "I didn't

say this stuff. Not in that context. You went through my phone? Most of those texts were to my sister, and the last one was to Jake. I'm not allowed to speak...intimately to my own mate?"

"That text wasn't to me," Jake argued.

"Lie. Shaky voice," Stark muttered as he thumbed through the pages.

Shit! She hadn't even seen him take the paperwork!

She reached for them but he leaned back so fast, he blurred out of her way. Dammit, he was quick!

"Who is Billy?" Stark asked, reading silently from page three or four.

"One of her boyfriends," Jake said.

"I don't even know a Billy!" Lyndi yelled.

"You will be quiet and we will have order in this meeting!" Abner yelled, slamming his fist on the table.

Stark didn't even react, just kept reading the damning papers.

"And this next boyfriend is supposed to be Jack?" he asked. He arched an eyebrow at Jake. "Someone needs to take lessons on coming up with more creative names. Or maybe it was just easier to photoshop the names in a text if it was close to your own name. Although gross to the sheer number of times she asked if she could get you food, or if you wanted to spend time with her after she got off work. Terrible mate, ech. I like your responses though. Can't get much colder, man."

"Those aren't my responses! Those are text messages with her boyfriends. Multiple boyfriends!"

"Shaky voice, for you idiots in the room who missed the lies," Stark said nonchalantly as he leaned back on the back two legs of his chair.

Lyndi's cheeks were on fire, her ears were on fire—she was embarrassed and enraged and hurt and betrayed, and she couldn't conjure up even a single word to defend herself.

"She kicked me out of the house multiple times," Jake said.

His representative murmured Jake's name and shook his head.

Jake ignored him and said, "She was cold in our bed!"

"Probably because you have a gross penis," Stark said, turning the page.

"Enough!" Abner yelled.

The roaring in her ears was getting to be too

much, and her fox was clawing to get out.

"She can't have kits," Jake's mother, Marsha, said.

The betrayal.

The room went silent. Dead quiet. The footstep of a mouse would've been deafening in this moment. Stark had frozen beside her, and inside, the fox was scratching at her skin to break free. To run away and never come back.

"What do you mean?" Abner asked.

"She cheated, and she kicked him out over and over, and didn't want to sleep with him because she couldn't have kits. They tried for five years. My son deserves to carry on our name and the family genetics, for the benefit of our community." Marsha looked directly at Lyndi with such hatred in her eyes. "Lyndi Mosley is a valueless cull fox, and we were all tricked by her."

She'd been stabbed. That's what it felt like. The words "cull fox" echoed around in her brain, like Marsha had shouted them from the ledge of the Grand Canyon.

She dared a look at Stark, and his eyes were wide and glued to her. "Do you want me to kill them?" he whispered in a voice so sincere, she knew that if she said yes, none of them would leave this room alive.

Her lip trembled, and her eyes burned, but she shook her head slowly. "I think I'm going to Change soon."

"Okay. Do *you* want to kill them?" he asked softly.

"I don't think we should kill anyone today."

She'd never seen a look of such utter disappointment on a man's face before. If she didn't feel drunk with grief, it would've probably struck her as funny. Stark had always been a delinquent.

Stark lifted his voice, "My client would like to be untethered from that douche canoe."

"It's called unpairing, and I requested it first," Jake said. "I'm the one going back into the breeding pool, I'm the viable—"

"Shut the fuck up," Stark said. "Lyndi told me about your micropenis and your erectile dysfunction problems and how you suck your thumb at nights when you're feeling insecure."

"What? None of that is true, he's lying."

"You do have a very small penis," Lyndi said numbly. "It's like the size of a peanut shell. But not a big two-peanut shell. One with only one peanut in it."

Stark laughed and held up the stapled papers of

her supposed crimes. "Can I take this home? I want to make fun of y'all with my Pack."

"This is completely inappropriate," Igor uttered.

Lyndi stood, and now the tears were flowing, and that made her angry. She wiped them off and pointed a finger at Igor. "You approved of us. You saw how happy we were. And you see him now. You can't sit there and tell me that awful man is the man you met five years ago. Who does this to a mate?"

Igor swallowed hard and looked at the table, shook his head.

"I'll sign whatever you want me to sign. I don't really care about being a part of this community anymore." She couldn't believe she'd just said that. Couldn't believe those words had fallen from her mouth.

Being a fox shifter was the most important thing about her.

Abner pushed a single paper to the edge of his table. It was an easy read. It dissolved their pairing completely. She signed it with the ink pen he handed her. Drew her name so hard onto that damn paper, it probably scratched the letters into the wooden table underneath.

Entire body shaking, she looked at Jake and his traitor family, and then to the council members. "Best of luck breeding that one."

And then she turned, and Stark was there, right behind her, tall and strong as an oak tree, steady, a safe spot in a room of liars.

He'd had her back, and he didn't even have any eggs in this basket. The Lost Wolf was better than any of these people she'd looked up to in here.

There was a soft growl in his throat, but he opened the door for her and left the room easy enough.

He muttered something so softly to the people in that room, she didn't quite understand it.

"See you real soon."

She'd probably misheard him. "What did you say?" she asked the furious-looking monster who walked beside her down the hall.

"Oh, I just said it's almost noon."

Lie, but he didn't seem to care.

He opened the door for her, and without a word, he wrapped his strong hand around hers and dragged her through the parking lot.

Lyndi was falling apart, and her legs weren't

working right.

Cull fox.

Cull fox.

Valueless cull fox.

"Three minutes," he murmured.

But she didn't understand. Human words were hard to understand right now because the fox was filling her head.

He helped her into the truck and slammed the door closed, then jumped in and fired up his roaring engine, and they were off.

Her skin tingled and she pulled at her clothes because they were too tight, too tight.

"Stark," she struggled out...

"I know," he rumbled, and pulled them off a main street and onto a one-lane dirt road.

He was flying. The woods blurred by and Lyndi was breaking apart. "I can't stop it," she said in a strangled voice.

"You don't have to." Stark slammed on his brakes and threw it into park, then reached across her and pulled the handle of her door.

And the last thing she remembered before the fox took her body was Stark's handsome face and bright-blue wolf eyes, staring at her with such care—like she was actually important.

He said two words as her body broke.

"You're free."

FIVE

Stark had never been to Promise Falls before now. Daylen had named the new Pack the Promise Falls Pack because it meant something to him and Denver, but this was the first time Stark had actually laid eyes on it.

Lyndi had led him here, to this rickety old bench, overlooking a river with a waterfall across the waves.

He didn't get chills in general, but when he looked down at the bench, two names caught his attention, and lifted gooseflesh on his arms. 'Lyndi and Jake' had been carved into the seat. Now he tried not to get too sentimental about it, because the words 'Farts for Sale' and 'Beans are Not the Magical Fruit' had also been carved into the bench, but still, the sight of

Jake's name dredged up some feelings he didn't understand. Anger was the biggest one.

That idiot had come here with Lyndi at some point and carved that with her. He dragged his gaze from that damned name to the fox that sat with her back to him, staring at the waterfall. She'd been sitting here for hours.

He'd imagined Lyndi was a red fox, with perfect patches of white, and black tips on her ears, mask, and legs. He'd been wrong.

Lyndi was a black fox, with patches of lighter gray on her face and sides. Her mask, ears, legs, and that fluffy tail were the color of night, and the only white on her was a small crest on her chest, and the tip of her tail.

Her gold eyes looked even brighter surrounded by all that dark.

He'd never seen anything like her.

For the first time in his life, he wished he could Change without wanting to fight. Fighting had fueled his wolf his entire life, but right now? He wished he was one of those normal werewolves who could control their animal completely. He wished he could Change into his wolf and go sit beside her and just be.

It felt more important than sitting here as a man. He didn't like the distance between them, but that didn't make any sense. He was only a few yards away from her.

Stark had plans for Jake.

He pulled out his oversized pocketknife and slammed it into the bench over Jake's name. Lyndi didn't flinch, only twisted around to look at him with hollow eyes. Stark dug Jake's name right out of that wood, took the handful of splinters, and chucked them into the water. He didn't want anything that slug had touched to be near any part of Lyndi.

He shoved his hands deep into his pockets as he stood beside the fox. It was getting dark, and though it was spring, the nights still got chilly here around Leadville. Was she warm enough? *Chhh. Of course she is. She's a fox. Got that pretty coat on.*

Why was he feeling the chill so harshly? Maybe because of the fight with Tessa. He was healing slow.

Tessa.

Stark had work to do, because he had a purpose now. He was going to make sure Lyndi was safe from everyone who had hurt her.

The fox sighed and looked up at him.

"I know," he murmured before he could stop himself. Stark dragged his gaze back to the waterfall. "I've been pushed out before, too. The sting won't go away, Lyndi, but you'll get stronger. You'll learn how to ignore the pain."

The scent of wolf drifted to him on the wind. Stark lifted his chin and sniffed the air. It was Daylen, and now he could smell Denver too.

She snapped a twig as she strode down the trail to them. Lyndi didn't even turn around as her sister approached.

"I got your message," Denver said, as Daylen hung back from the fox at the rivers' edge. "What happened?"

"Oh, she's having PMS or something," Stark said lightly. "Not my problem. Figured she needed girl time or some shit."

Stark cast Lyndi one last glance, and the fox was just staring at him with an unreadable expression on her pretty face. He sauntered toward the trail for the long walk back to his truck. He meant to walk straight off, but his Alpha was doing something that stopped him in his tracks.

Daylen was sitting on the bench, looking down at

where he'd just gutted the board with Jake's name on it. All that remained was the word 'Lyndi', and as Daylen moved to touch the disfigured carving, Stark couldn't stop the snarling words that crawled up the back of his throat. "Don't touch her name."

Daylen froze and dragged bright-gold eyes up to him. Stark wanted to fight him. For a loaded few seconds, he considered it. Everything had gotten so fucked up for Lyndi, and now he was on edge and couldn't stand anyone else messing with anything to do with her. Nope, he couldn't explain that instinct, and right now, he didn't care.

Daylen cocked his head, narrowed his eyes, and relaxed back against the seat. "What's going on, Stark?"

"That ain't my story to tell." Stark strode off in the direction of his truck.

"Where are you going?" Daylen called from behind him.

"To find Tessa."

SIX

3 MONTHS LATER...

"I brought Cheetos!" Denver sang as she barged into Lyndi's new apartment.

Lyndi laughed and plopped onto the garage-sale couch she'd picked up over the weekend for a hundred bucks. It was a little worn, but she'd just placed decorative pillows over the threadbare places and it was cute as heck in her small living room.

"You're the one who likes Cheetos, Denver. Not me."

"Oh yeah," Denver muttered remorselessly as she sank onto the old recliner Lyndi had picked up at Goodwill. She ripped open the bag with her teeth like an animal. "This is a big deal, Lyndi."

Lyndi's cheeks heated with pleasure. "I know," she said softly. "But then again, everything feels like a big deal lately."

"You hired your first server."

"I've hired a dozen servers for Zaps before," Lyndi said with a giggle.

"Yeah, but this is the first one you've hired since you're the official co-owner! I told Mom and Dad. They seemed proud!"

Lyndi's heart dropped at the mention of them. "Really?"

Denver inhaled deeply, and gave a too-bright smile. "I think they're coming around."

Lyndi snorted and pulled the remote she'd accidentally sat on out from underneath her. "I appreciate your lies. The council gave them a breakdown of all the paperwork and all of Jake's accusations, and now the entire community knows. Mom and Dad are shamed."

"So-the-frick-what?" Denver asked around a bite. "One of their other daughters is mated to a werewolf. I practically paved the way for you to branch off."

"Ha! By branch off, you mean fail a pairing, be

labeled barren, and be culled from the mating pool? Now our family will never live down the embarrassment. Branching off has been super fun."

Denver's smile had faded as she'd spoken, and her sister set the bag of chips onto the small coffee table in between them and rested her elbows on her knees. "That stuff isn't as important as you think, Lyndi."

"It was my whole life. Jake and that pairing were what I'd been prepped for my entire existence. I planned on forever, and it was a shock having that fall apart. Now what do I do? What's my purpose?"

"First off, your purpose wasn't ever to be a breeder for that dimwit Jake the Snake. I read the accusations, too—"

"Denver, you swore you wouldn't—"

"Well, I guess I've been lying about a lot of things."

"Like what?"

"Forget it," Denver said, looking down at her clenched hands. "Look...you saw your purpose differently than I ever saw for you. You're smart, and hardworking, and kind, and always there for people who need you. I always saw you as this person who

had all your shit together, even when we were kids—
"

"Ha! And now look at me."

"Yeah. Yeah, Lyndi, look at you." Denver arched her dark eyebrows high. "The joy of my life has been watching you pull yourself out of that hole over the last three months and find yourself and discover your independence again. Jake did some damage. I've loved watching you get stubborn and undo it. And even if you can't have babies—"

"Denver—"

"No, let me finish. Even if you can't? It's okay."

Lyndi couldn't look at her anymore. She couldn't. No one was supposed to know about any of this, no one was supposed to hear about what she and Jake had dealt with. This was her burden, and no one was invited to shoulder it with her.

"It's okay," Denver said softer. "Jake wasn't it. He was a douche from the start. If you find someone someday, and you want that? You want a kit? You want a family?" Denver pointed to herself. "I'll help. If I'm able, I'll carry a kit for you. I'll be a surrogate."

Lyndi's eyes were burning, and she bit her lip hard to stop the trembling there. She tried to speak, because that offer was big. It was potentially someday life-changing.

"Fuck, I'll make you a kit even if you never find anyone. Let's have a baby! We just need a sperm donor. I Googled it. Think of how pissed the council would be then, huh?" Denver leaned back into the recliner with a wicked smile. "A baby born and raised between the two of us. A black sheep badass bar-owning hottie and Second in a Pack of motherfreaking werewolves. That kid would be so cool. The council would cry themselves to sleep every night knowing he existed. In my mind I've already decided we are having a boy. We are naming him Hudson Wayne, and starting his UFC career at the age of three so he can grow up to kick Jake's ass for being terrible to you. I was thinking we should start with boxing and karate. What do you think?"

Lyndi laughed. That was one thing about Denver. She could always turn something hard into a joke and move them forward faster.

"Hudson Wayne sounds awesome." And the tears stayed sucked up in her eyeballs, because Denver had done what Denver always did; made her feel better.

"Yeah, and he can inherit the badass bar you just

became part owner of! Badass baby raised by a badass momma. Now keep doing the thing, Lyndi. Keep finding yourself because trust me, looking from the outside in? You're killing it."

"I have an admission," Lyndi said, fighting the feelings of guilt.

"Admit away."

"I don't miss him."

A slow smile spread across Denver's face. "By next year, he will feel like he existed in a different life."

"How's Stark?" she asked before she could tuck the question back inside of herself. She always chickened out, but not today.

Denver chewed on the side of her lip and studied Lyndi. "He's been away."

"Oh?" Lyndi cleared her throat and fidgeted with a loose thread on the throw pillow she'd dragged into her lap. "Away where?"

"We don't know. He only comes back to his RV a couple times a week. He disappeared for an entire month after you guys spent your secret-mission day together."

"Oh, come on, you aren't still mad about that."

"You didn't tell me you were going in front of the council, but you told Stark."

Lyndi shrugged up one shoulder. "Stark felt safe to tell."

"On what planet would Stark be a safe place for anything?"

"He was kind to me. In his own way."

"Stark and kind don't belong in the same sentence. Dominant, rough around the edges, stubborn, forceful, inappropriate at any serious occasion, brawling madman is a good description."

Lyndi parted her lips to defend Stark, but a knock pounded on the door and startled her. She yelped and stood in a rush.

"Expecting anyone?" Denver asked.

"No, just you today. The fox is protective of the new den. I can't invite anyone else over yet."

Lyndi stood and made her way to the door, then pushed aside the blue curtains from the window to see outside. Jake stood on her doorstep, looking furious.

Lyndi gasped and dropped the curtain. She hadn't seen him since the meeting with the council. "It's Jake," she whispered.

"Tell him to go eat a dick," Denver advised her. "A gross one."

"I can hear you in there," Jake called through the door.

The fox inside of her was scrabbling to get out, and her skin was starting to tingle with rage. Lyndi threw open the door. "What do you want?"

"Call your guard dog off."

That was a word combination she never thought she would hear out of his mouth, so she paused for a few moments before her response. Jake looked different. He looked skinnier, and his face was sunken. The blue in his eyes was duller, and he had dark circles now. He looked unkempt, and unwashed and exhausted down to his bones. "You look like shit."

"Yeah? Shocker, Lyndi. Maybe it's because you sicced that psychopath on me and my parents, and we haven't slept in three fucking months. Call. Him. Off."

Guard dog? "Who are you talking about?"

"That werewolf you brought to the meeting!" he yelled, gripping his hair. "All night long, he howls, and he gets closer and closer and closer. A month ago, he started scratching at the doors. There are claw marks all over my parents' house! I can hear him growling. He's always growling. I'm even dreaming about it! We had to put more locks on the house, but I know he gets in there. I come home and furniture is moved and it smells like wolf, but he never takes anything. He doesn't do anything but torture us. Every day. Every night. We thought he would give up and move on but no. He'll never leave me alone. Lyndi, I'm asking you, if you ever had a care in your heart for me, you'll ask him to give us peace."

Never in her life had Lyndi felt so shocked. Behind her, Denver laughed. "So that's where he's been. That's awesome."

"How is this awesome?" Jake demanded. "I've handled this split in a very mature manner—"

"Did you?" Lyndi asked, stepping outside onto the welcome mat. Jake took a step back. At least the moron had some smarts, because Lyndi was shaking mad. "How dare you come here, to my new den that I had to *scratch* for, and demand favors from me. Barren Whore Admissions: if that werewolf killed you, I wouldn't be sad. Get the fuck off my lawn. You smell like beef jerky and desperation."

Jake clenched his fists at his sides, and his eyes

blazed the gold of his fox. Red crept up his neck and into his cheeks. She'd seen him this angry before and had hated it.

Denver appeared beside her, held up a spray can of Febreze, and pulled the little trigger. A fine mist of berry-and-bramble scented fog engulfed Jake's face. "Begone, demon."

Jake coughed and backed up, rubbing his eyes. "What the hell, Denver!"

"Make haste," she called after him. "Before I call the guard dog. Methinks he wouldn't like you stepping foot near the princess's moat!"

Jake was almost to his car, one hand shoved deep in his pockets, one hand rubbing his watering eyes, muttering curses. And Lyndi? Lyndi was trying to control the giggles that were bubbling straight up her throat.

Stark had been avenging her.

"Oh my gosh," she whispered to Denver. "Stark has been messing with Jake for three months?"

"Apparently," Denver said through her cackling. "What a thorn! Oh my God, I was wondering why he was less annoying lately. He's too tired to bug us." She burst out into maniacal laughter.

"I don't understand," Lyndi murmured as she watched Jake peel out of her driveway. "Stark hasn't said a single word to me since that day. I tried to call him to thank him for being there for me, but he never answered and never called back. I even left messages. I thought he hated me or something."

"Oh, no, he doesn't hate you. Here, check your phone," she said, poking around on hers.

"Okaaay." Lyndi's phone vibrated and she checked the text that came through from Denver. It was a picture, and what she saw in it stunned her. It was an image of her dark fox sitting by the river, and Stark standing on the shore next to her, his hands shoved deep into his pockets, his eyes on her. The photo dredged up chills across her entire body. The way he was looking at her...he didn't hate her at all.

Denver told her, "Daylen ordered him to stay away from you."

"What?" Lyndi yelped.

"Well, technically I asked Daylen to order Stark to stay away from you, but for good reason."

"What could possibly be the reason, Denver?" Lyndi admonished her. "Stark was a very good friend to me and you cut us off. Why did you do that? I've

73

been so confused for the last three months."

"Because Stark asked us how much time you needed." Denver's tone had turned serious and the smile had faded from her lips.

"How much time I needed?" she whispered, baffled. "What does that mean?"

"It means he was showing too much interest, too soon. Stark is a hunter, Lyndi. You were going through something huge and he is the king of getting in people's heads. I didn't want him stunting your progress. You're a phoenix! Where are you going?"

Lyndi grabbed her keys and the closest pair of shoes she could find, which happened to be a pair of rubber mud boots with little gray chickens printed all over them. Sexy. She shoved her feet into them and gritted out, "I'm going to go find my *friend* and finally thank him for being there for me that day, like I tried to do three months ago."

"Your head wasn't clear then."

"It's plenty clear now."

"Lyndi!"

"Denver," she growled, rounding on her sister. "I'm grown. I'm over Jake, and I've accepted my fate as a lone fox. One of the only benefits to being cast out like this is I can be friends with whomever I want, and that includes delinquent werewolves with disappearing problems. No. More. Meddling."

The smile returned to Denver's lips, but that just confused Lyndi more. She frowned at her sister and jogged to her trusty old Honda Accord.

"Don't you need to lock the house?" Denver called after her.

"Don't pretend you didn't already make a spare key, you stage five clinger," Lyndi called.

Denver grinned. "I'll lock up then."

Lyndi hid a smile as she turned her car on and backed out of the driveway. She wasn't headed to find Stark just yet. She needed to get to the root of the problem first, and that root was named Daylen Hoda.

SEVEN

Stark was a dead man walking.

At least that's how he felt. Right about now, he could out-zombie an actual zombie. He'd worked late for the boss after the other roofers had gone home, and he'd finished a house by himself. Tomorrow, they could start another house instead of spending a half-day on the last job.

Gerald had already texted him and thanked him for staying late, and said he'd earned a morning to sleep in. Hell yeah he did, he'd been working every day for the last couple months, trying to keep steady. His life was all about routine now—work all day, eat when he could, Change into the wolf and run Jake's family territory at nights, try to function on little to no sleep, repeat the next day.

All so he could keep Lyndi out of his head.

Fuck Daylen for his dumb order. Stark needed to move on soon. Being a lone wolf would hurt the animal, but sometimes he thought that was the only way he could exist and find any peace. Just leave the Pack behind and live for himself. It was the damn wolf that kept him chasing Packs. He needed friends, apparently. Stupid animal just wanted to fight his friends though. God, he was so broken.

In a daze, Stark gassed his truck up the last hill to Daylen's territory. Now it felt like his territory too, which he would have to change soon. He needed to buy some land to park his RV on, land that didn't smell like other dominant male wolves. He wanted to kill Daylen most days now.

And speak of the devil himself, Daylen was standing on the crest of the hill with his arms crossed, blocking the road.

Stark slammed on his brakes just to make sure the cloud of gravel dust coated his Alpha completely. Daylen didn't look amused as the dust settled.

Stark rolled down his window. "What did I do wrong now?" he barked.

Daylen approached his window, and a snarl ripped out of Stark. "Look, I'm tired as hell and I don't have it in me to get a lecture right now, so if you're—"

"You can see Lyndi now." The soft tone of Daylen's voice drifted right through Stark and settled in his bones.

"What happened?" Stark asked.

"She came to see me."

"Lyndi did?" Stark asked, hope blooming in his chest.

"Yep. I'm lifting the order at her request." Daylen patted the open window frame twice. "Don't fuck this up, okay? She's been through enough."

He hated the look on Daylen's face. It was a mixture of defeat and disappointment.

"I'm not that bad, you know," Stark gritted out.

"You're not that good either." Daylen held his gaze a moment longer before he climbed back up the hill and disappeared.

Stark leaned his head back on the headrest and sighed as he studied the leaf-covered branches that overhung the gravel road. He could see Lyndi again. Maybe the wolf would give him a break if he could make sure she was really all right. Maybe he could stop thinking about her if he knew she was fine and moving forward.

He eased his boot onto the gas and crested that final length of drive to see Lyndi's Accord parked in front of his RV.

His heart stuttered in his chest cavity and he perked up. She opened the driver's side door and time slowed as she got out. Lyndi was wearing skintight leggings, a blue-and-black flannel jacket, and chicken-printed rain boots. Her hair was wavy and wild, lifting in the breeze as she angled her face to him. Stunning gold-rimmed eyes. Pink cheeks. High cheekbones. The smile that ghosted her lips steadied out his heartbeat, then sent it to galloping and *oh shit.* The wolf inside of him was completely zeroed in on her. *There she is.*

Nothing else existed right now.

He parked the truck where it was and got out. Stunned, he sauntered over to her and she met him in the middle.

She stopped a few feet shy and he followed suit, unable to take his eyes from hers.

"I know what you did," she said. "I know what you've been doing. Jake told me."

Her chest lifted and fell with her fast breaths, and he thought he'd done something wrong. Thought she was angry...until she threw her arms over his shoulders and held on like he was a life raft. "Thank you," she whispered against his ear.

The tension left his body as he slid his hands to her waist and gripped her shirt there, then wrapped his arms around her middle and dragged her in even closer.

A hug. That's what this was. Were hugs supposed to feel like this? Were they supposed to make everything about a life make sense for a few moments?

Her hand went to the back of his head and her nails scratched his scalp gently, conjuring ripples of chills all over his body.

With a soft groan, he lifted her off the ground, buried his face into the side of her neck, and inhaled deeply to memorize her scent. Fuck what that said about him. He didn't care how bad everyone thought he was. He wouldn't let anyone hurt Lyndi, and that's all that mattered to a creature like him. Could he make her safe? Yes. The rest he would have to figure out as he went along.

"I'm tired," he uttered in a gravelly voice. He didn't know why he'd admitted that, but the words had just tumbled out. The pull of exhaustion crashed down on him. Stark settled her onto her feet, but left his hands resting on her waist. She was cupping his cheeks, studying his face.

"You did good." Her eyes were the color of good whiskey now, and he could smell the faint scent of her animal. "It's time for rest, okay?"

He nodded. He would do anything she asked right now. She pulled his hand and led him to the RV, and waited by the stairs as he climbed them. With the door swung open, he turned, and twitched his head for her to come join him.

"I know better than to come into a wolf den," she said, a soft smile in her words.

"I won't put any moves on you. You'll be safe in the den. Can you stay a while?"

She looked so pretty, her little pixie nose tipped up in the air as she blushed. A slight nod, and she climbed the stairs behind him.

And now Lyndi was right where he wanted her.

EIGHT

Stark's RV was fancy.

Lyndi stepped inside and was immediately weighed down with the heaviness of dominance and the smell of wolf. She froze.

"The wolf won't let anything happen to you," Stark said from where he was leaning against the kitchen island. His eyes were the storm blue that said his wolf wasn't at the surface right now. His cheekbones were a little sharper than she remembered, and his muscles more cut. He was taller, but maybe she'd just forgotten how big he felt when she was in his presence. His blond mohawk was down and flipped to the side, only covering part of his face. The other side was buzzed short. A light blue T-shirt clung to his broad shoulders, and his work jeans sat low on his hips. The look in his eyes was pure exhaustion, and it pulled at her heartstrings. "When was the last time you slept through the night?" she asked.

"The night before the council meeting," he uttered, no hesitation.

Stark was special. She didn't understand the reasons he'd spent so much time and energy hurting the people who had hurt her, but she knew he was bigger than she'd realized.

There was a trio of stairs and down a short hallway, she could see the foot of a bed. She grinned and pointed her finger. "To bed."

Stark cast a quick look up to the bedroom, then back to her. "I don't want you to leave. I can stay awake."

"Go," she ordered, pushing on his lower back gently. Now, every fiber of her being knew that if Stark didn't want to be moved it would take a tsunami to make him budge, but he was pliable enough under her touch. Up the stairs he went, and he sat on the bed. As he pressed the toe of one boot against the heel of the other to shed it, she knelt in front of him and shook her head.

Slowly, she untied his boot and pulled it off, then his sock, and then did the same for the other. Boots lined neatly against the wall beside his other pair, she returned and leaned down, pulled the hem of his T-shirt straight over his head as he lifted his arms to help her.

His hair was mussed and sexy. She ran her hands through it to rough it up, nails gentle on his scalp. He let off a low growl. His hands went to the backs of her knees and he pulled her in between his legs. The giant was almost as tall sitting on his bed as she was standing in front of him.

Lyndi should be nervous, right? She should have flutters of fear, and a fox who was clawing to run away from the big bad wolf, but this felt like the most natural thing that had ever happened in her life.

She dragged both hands over his head to smooth back his mohawk and angled his face right at her. "I'm nothing to them now," she murmured, because he should know she'd been shamed and shunned by her own people.

The blue in his eyes lightened, and his lips quirked up into a crooked smile. "Good. Then you're a

Lost Fox."

She guessed that nickname was a compliment from the Lost Wolf.

"Do you want to be friends with me?" she asked.

"I don't do labels," he said softly.

"You're just a walking red flag, aren't you?"

"Red is my favorite color."

Danger, danger, danger. This man wasn't something to mess with.

"I'll tell you what I'll do," he said. "I'll make sure you're safe to live your life exactly how you want to. You don't have to look over your shoulder or worry about what people think of you. No one will harm you. You can build whatever life you want to as a lone fox. No one will have anything to say about it, or they can deal with me. I'll be whatever that means."

That sounded like more than friends to her, but if he was a man who hated labels, he wouldn't appreciate her pointing that out.

"Why would you do all of this for me?" she asked.

"Because the wolf requires it," Stark answered simply.

Huh.

"I'll repay you."

"You already have."

Lyndi frowned. "How?"

Stark's light-blue eyes swam with an earnestness as he told her, "You gave the animal a purpose."

She had to think about all of this. She needed time. Stark was very different than she'd thought for all this time, and he was intriguing her in a way that felt scary—like her toes were on the edge of a diving board, but the pool beneath her was full of murky water and she couldn't tell how deep it was. This could feel like a triumph, or hurt a great deal.

Lyndi stepped back out of the space he'd created between his knees for her and made her way to the head of the bed. She folded down the comforter and gestured for him to get in.

He looked puzzled. Troubled even, perhaps. "I scared you."

Lyndi shook her head. "I don't know you well enough to give you purpose."

Three breaths of silence passed before he laid back on top of the comforter she'd pulled back. "Covers make me feel trapped."

"You never sleep with covers on?" Strange. Covers were supposed to be a comfort, not a cage.

"Don't you get cold?"

"No."

He laid on his side. He was so tall, his ankles hung off the mattress. His tan skin said he'd been working outside in the spring sunshine, and his abs flexed with every breath. Everything, down the long claw mark scars on his body, was perfect. At least to her, it was.

When she dragged her eyes back to his face, a faint, devilish smile clung to the corners of his lips. "Forget what I said about purpose. It was a mistake. If you want to pay me back, you can anytime you want."

The grin got bigger, and she shoved his arm, well aware of what he meant. "I'm not trading sex for protection."

Stark adjusted the hard bulge of his erection between his legs. "You were the one who was just looking at me like you want to eat me. Do you want to eat me, Lost Fox?"

"You're dangerous," she murmured, stepping back.

"To everyone else. Not to you."

One last glance at his powerful body, and the heat was back in her cheeks. "I don't know what I'm doing here. You need rest, and I should go."

"I'll rest better if you're here." The wicked glint had left his face, and a vulnerability she didn't understand took its place. "Stay."

"Only if you promise to leave Jake and his family alone for a couple of weeks."

Stark clenched his teeth. "You still have feelings for him?"

"No. He could fall in the lake and never resurface and I wouldn't care. I want you to leave him alone because vengeance is a poison. If you drink it for too long, you can't go back, Stark. It will change you."

"You're scared of change?"

Lyndi shook her head slowly. "No. Not much scares me anymore. But today I learned you have been the steadiest thing about my life over the last three months, and I wasn't even aware." She cocked her head. "I don't want you to change. I don't want you to *need* vengeance. Jake wins if you go dark."

"You're good, aren't you?" he asked in a hoarse, exhausted voice. "Those are the kind of things good people say. They don't make any difference to men like me. Jake is the last thing I have to hunt here."

Lyndi bit her bottom lip to hide a smile, because

she knew she was about to say something she couldn't take back—not with Stark.

"Hunt me, then."

Stark's eyes flashed brighter, and a wave of raw power and desire drifted from him. God, he was beautiful, if a brawler could be called that.

"Stay," he murmured.

"Sleep," she whispered, making no promises.

And then she padded softly to the door, hit the button for the lights, and made her way down the stairs to the door.

After a minute of hesitation, she went against what a good fox was *supposed* to do, and did what she *wanted* to do.

Lyndi passed by the door, sat on the couch and dragged the blanket from the back over her lap, and waited.

"Thank you," came the tired murmur from the other room, just before his breathing slowed and deepened with sleep.

Heart fluttering with all that had just happened between her and Stark, she pulled her phone out and opened a text to Denver.

I want to join your Pack. Send.

If she was going to hell, she may as well have an adventure getting there.

NINE

"Lyndi."

That voice sounded so familiar. Her whispered name tickled the inside of her head. Flashes of unfamiliar forest rolled through her mind like lightning. The sound of her labored panting was deafening, punctuated by the pounding of her heartbeat.

She was scared.

Ahead of her, another fox was running. A red fox. The fox turned to check if Lyndi was still behind her. Denver?

Wait! Slow down, I'm not chasing you.

Something big ran through the trees beside her, so fast she could only see the blur of fur. It was much bigger than her. Wolf.

Oh my gosh! *Lyndi tucked her tail and ran even faster, desperate to catch up to Denver. The woods weren't flashing like slideshow pictures anymore. They were solid. They were real. The wind was real on her fur, and she flattened her ears back and cried out as she lost sight of Denver ahead of her.*

Something big was behind her. A snarl rippled through the air, and then another. In the distance, a howl pierced the night sky.

Denver!

Lyndi panicked. She ducked under fern leaves and vaulted over tree roots, faster and faster...

She skidded out of thick foliage and there was Denver. The red fox was waiting up ahead beside a huge tree whose roots were rolling out of the ground like waves.

Denver had her ears pinned back, staring in horror at something behind Lyndi. The fur down her spine was raised in fear, prickling her skin. Run, run, don't look back! *At the last second, Denver ducked into a deep den hole under the tree. With a yelp, Lyndi followed.*

The sound of their panting filled the small, dark space, and Denver maneuvered them, pressing them as far back into the hole as she could. Denver put herself in front of Lyndi, and when she turned and looked at Lyndi, her gold eyes were filled with terror.

And then the teeth appeared, and the gray-colored wolf ripped Denver out of the den. She would never forget Denver's screech of pain, or the sound of ripping as Lyndi jumped out after her.

"Denver!" Lyndi shrieked, sitting up in the dark.

She couldn't see anything. She was in the den again. She was in the den! A soft growling vibrated through the air and froze her into place.

Breath shaking, Lyndi eased her eyes over to the pair of glowing blue eyes. His snarling, gravelly voice cut through the darkness. "Tessa is building a new Pack."

Lyndi flew off the couch and crouched on the floor, a growl in her throat.

"It's me, Stark," came the rumbling voice. He flipped the lights on, and there he was, clad in sweats and no shirt, his chest glistening with sweat that trickled down to his abs. Rage still simmered in his ice-blue eyes, but his words were gentle. "You're safe."

"I...I had a dream," she uttered in a trembling

voice.

"I saw it. I had the same one. I was in those woods, too, but the pack had pulled Daylen and me off. Marsden..." Stark swallowed hard. "We were trying to get to you. Couldn't. It wasn't real, Lyndi. None of it was real. Tessa just used old pack bonds to fuck with us. She imagined all of that."

"But why did I see that? Why was I a part of it? I saw Denver. She killed Denver. I was there. I saw Tessa grab her. I heard Tessa killing her. How the hell can Tessa be in my head? I'm not Pack."

A soft knock rapped on the door and Lyndi jumped. Stark, however, was already reaching to open the door.

Daylen stood on the other side, and behind him, Denver. Both of them looked as haunted as Lyndi felt. She bolted for Denver and nearly bowled them both over as she hugged her up in the yard.

"I know," Denver whispered. "It's okay. It's okay. She didn't get me; it was made up."

"You protected me. Denver, I could control my body in that dream." She eased her sister back to arm's length. "That is some dark magic."

"Tessa's..." Denver pursed her lips. "Tessa's a

problem. She was always an extremist for power, but since Vager died, I think she's not all there anymore. All she has is this."

"What is this?"

"Revenge, I suppose. Daylen kicked her out of his pack, and I had my run-in with her, and then Stark did his thing."

Lyndi frowned and cast a quick glance up at the trailer, where the door had swung closed. She could hear the boys talking quietly inside. In a whisper, she asked, "What did Stark do?"

Now it was Denver's turn to purse her lips. "He made sure she wasn't around here to bother you anymore. That's where he was the first month after your meeting with the council."

"But..." Lyndi shook her head in shock. "Why would he do that for me?"

Denver shrugged up one shoulder. "I think that's a question for Stark. Who really knows what that man is thinking? I can guess, but it might be wrong."

"Guess."

Denver huffed a soft laugh. "No more meddling from me, remember?"

Touché.

Car lights shone over the yard as an old, jacked-up Jeep Grand Cherokee crested the hill. Lyndi tensed, but Denver rested her hand on her arm. "It's Marsden."

He rocked to a stop and shoved the door open, and the giant werewolf said, "I just had the most fucked-up dream. Stark!" he yelled as he stomped up the stairs. "Why the fuck did you let me die?"

"Because you are the least useful member of the Pack—" *crash!* The fifth wheel rocked to the side so drastically, it went up on one side and nearly tipped over before it settled back upright. There was lots of yelling, and some colorful swear words.

"Oh God," Denver muttered, pulling Lyndi by the arm five feet to the left of the door. Exactly two seconds later, Stark tossed Marsden out of his RV, and the behemoth hit the dirt just where they'd been standing, hard enough to make a small crater.

The ground cracked and the split travelled right under the tires of the RV, causing it to sink down by a foot and settle completely crooked.

Marsden jumped up out of the hole he'd made with his body and jammed his finger at Stark, whose furious face had just appeared in the doorway to check the damage at the tire. "I shouldn't even be surprised that you let them kill me. You've always been a selfish prick!"

"You're the one who is mad at me for something that happened in a dream, you fucking girl!"

Lyndi cocked her head. "I'm slightly offended."

"Fasten up your girdle, sis," Denver told her. "They'll say way stupider stuff once they get going."

Stark jumped straight over all the stairs, and pointed to the crooked RV. "I would demand you haul my house back to level ground, but your shit-bucket doesn't have the power!"

Marsden's mouth fell open. "I drive a fine piece of well-made machinery that probably gets ten miles to the gallon more than your dumb, fancy new truck. Why don't you go wash it again, for the fourth time this week, Stark? Who are you trying to impress with that, anyway?"

"I'm impressed," Lyndi muttered under her breath, raising her hand.

"Ha!" Stark said, his laugh echoing down the mountain. "Who could you possibly impress with your dumpster? Only girl you ever had in that is the squirrel that lives under the back seat. And even

Brenda the Squirrel says it smells like beer and eggs in there, and she's looking for a new house. Rumor has it she thinks the soup at the bottom of a trash can would be more comfortable!"

Lyndi looked to Denver for help. Were they supposed to give in to their laughter, or no?

Marsden's eyes were bright green now, and his hands were clenched at his sides. "Take it back."

Stark enunciated each word. "Fuuuck. Youuu."

"Take it back or I will tip your goddamn house right over!"

"Fine." Stark crossed his arms. "Your car squirrel is happy with the nest she's made of empty Cheetos packages and empty juice boxes."

Daylen appeared in the open doorway of the RV, looking exhausted. He shook his head and jogged down the four stairs, then made his way to Lyndi and Denver. "Let's get out of their way."

"You want to order them to stop fighting?" Denver asked as the yelling continued.

"Absolutely not. Maybe they'll kill each other and then that's two fewer headaches for me. I'm going to bed. We can talk about what we're doing about Tessa tomorrow."

"Are all werewolf Packs like this?" Lyndi whispered.

"Nope," Denver drawled out. "We're one of a kind."

She turned to leave but Lyndi stopped her. "Hey, why does Tessa have access to my head?"

"That one I can't answer. My guess is it has something to do with Stark. But then again..." Denver arched her dark eyebrows at her. "You did text me that you wanted to be part of the Pack. Welcome to the shit show."

"Yeah, but isn't there some kind of ceremony or something?" she asked, following behind Denver and Daylen. "Like a full-moon party, or I don't know. Does one of you bite me and everyone drinks my blood and then I can make you have dreams too?"

"Hell no," Daylen muttered. "This isn't a vampire coven and none of us want any extra dreams. Tessa isn't even supposed to use bonds like that. It's against the rules."

"Okay, so where do I stand? Am I part of the Pack since I can see her dreams?"

"Lyndi, we will figure this all out in the morning," Daylen muttered.

Lyndi clenched her fists so hard, her nails dug into her palm. "Stop."

Daylen and Denver halted and turned to her.

"My whole life has been up in the air over the last few months, and for several years before that, I always got put off, and put off, and put off. I don't want to feel put off anymore. It's my least favorite feeling."

She hadn't been able to lift her eyes from the ground, but now she ghosted a glance at Daylen. His strong jaw was clenched, and his eyes lightened to gold. "Fuck Jake and your people for making you feel like you didn't belong, but this is a layered and complicated request, and I need time to think about it."

"I would be good. I would contribute. Denver told me you are looking to expand the Pack, and I know I'm not a wolf, but I can learn the dynamics. I'm a lone fox with no ties anymore. Denver is happy and has learned her niche and I guess I want that too, with people who won't judge me."

"Here is the reality," Daylen told her. "We have the smallest Pack in North America now, because all the others left right before I inherited this Pack. I have two delinquents as the only males here," he said, twitching his chin toward the now-brawling men behind them. "I have Tessa building an army and they don't mean us well, and I have your sister to protect. And on top of all of that, Stark has an interest in you that I don't understand. When he hurts you, and he will, what then? You'll be stuck in a small Pack with him."

"And what if he doesn't hurt me?" Lyndi asked stubbornly, because she was starting to realize Daylen didn't understand Stark at all. He didn't understand that Stark had chased away Tessa to keep Lyndi safe, or all the nights he spent exhausting himself just to punish Jake and his family on her behalf.

"If you think that, you have terrible taste in men."

Anger boiled through her blood. "I used to think Denver had bad taste in men until I got to know you. Then I turned into a cheerleader for you two. Maybe you should get to know Stark. Who knows? Maybe getting to know your wolves will make you a better Alpha." She let her pissed-off glare linger on Daylen for another couple of moments. Daylen was being smart. He was. She was stung because that was her trigger, but that was her problem, not his. He was Alpha here and what he said went.

She sighed. "I would actually like you to think about it and make a good and thoughtful decision rather than just let me in on the family card." She allowed a little smile. "Plus, if you do choose me for the Pack, I want to know I earned it. Just throw me in the hat with the others you are looking at adding. Fox, wolf, bear, or badger, I'll fight them all. I might as well use this ol' chip on my shoulder for something."

Denver was smiling now, and Lyndi gave her a wink before she turned and hiked back toward her car.

Stark and Marsden weren't fighting anymore. Instead, they were sitting on a couple of neon-orange camp chairs, staring at the lopsided RV and drinking matching orange juices.

"You can't leave yet," Stark called to her, dragging a hot-pink plastic chair closer to his and patting the seat.

"It's the middle of the night—"

"Ten p.m.," Stark corrected her.

"You're supposed to be sleeping—"

"I just got the best sleep of my life—"

"Because he killed me in his dream," Marsden muttered.

Stark ignored him and continued, "And plus I got you an orange juice, and every good guest knows you should never say no to a cold OJ."

Well, how could she say no to that? With a put-upon sigh to hide her amusement, she trudged over to the eye-scorching pink chair and sank into it. Stark leaned over and picked up a blanket off the ground that he must've brought out, laid it across her lap, and then leaned back in his chair and handed her an orange juice.

"To new friends," Stark said with a wicked smile.

Marsden smashed his drink against Stark's and spilled about half of it. "I'm not your friend," he announced, and then chugged the rest of his, threw down the empty plastic container, and kicked it so hard, it dinged against the side of Stark's RV. "That's for calling my rig trash."

"Tell Brenda hi from me," Stark called.

"I hate this Pack," Marsden said right before he slammed his door closed and revved the engine.

"You two seem to be real good buddies," she said sarcastically as she unscrewed the lid to her drink.

"Oh, he's harmless unless he has a tomahawk."

She had absolutely no idea how to respond to that, so she took a drink instead and nearly choked on the fiery flavor. She spit it out and croaked out, "What is that?"

"It's fireball and orange juice. It's a mimosa, and chicks dig mimosas. I Googled it."

Between coughing and hacking, she punched out, "That's not what a mimosa is at all."

Stark nodded. "You're welcome. I can make you pancakes when you get hungry."

"Do they have alcohol in them?"

"Maybe. Okay, go."

"Go what?"

"Tell me everything you want to tell me about yourself and I will listen."

Lyndi blinked hard. "I can't tell if you're being serious."

"You said we don't know each other yet, so here we go." He waved his fingers in the air. "I'm ready."

Lyndi giggled and dragged her knees to her chest so she could curl up in the chair better. "That's not how getting to know each other works. Why don't you try telling me about yourself?"

Stark narrowed his eyes. "That wasn't part of the deal."

"Then we remain strangers." She offered her hand for a shake. "Hi, my name is Lyndi Mosley. Nice to meet you, stranger."

Stark still looked hot, even with a scrunched-up face. "You may ask me one question."

Lyndi tapped her finger thoughtfully on the side of her face and searched for the perfect question that would start to make Stark make sense to her. Best start at the beginning. "Are you still close to your parents?"

"I will tell you about a pet turtle I had when I was five instead."

Hmm, he was going to be a tough one to open up. "Okay."

"I ate it. My turn. When is your birthday?"

"May fifteenth. You ate your own pet?"

"Yes. My turn again."

"No, no, no, you aren't really answering any of my questions well. Re-do. Why did you eat a turtle?"

"Because my wolf was hungry." He waited. "I felt a little bad about it afterward when I only had an empty tank left. I think I ate him because my uncle gave him to me and my uncle is a douchebag and I didn't like him, and so I ate his present."

"Poor turtle."

"Yessss. The turtle was definitely the worst thing I've ever done."

"Ha! I know you didn't max out at age five. And okay! I eat prey when I'm the fox. Turtles aren't my favorite, but to each his own."

Stark cocked his head and his bright-blue eyes bore straight into her soul. "What's your favorite?"

She froze. This was taboo, right? They weren't supposed to talk about their animal natures and what was done in the woods at night to sate their hunting instincts. "My favorite prey?"

"Yes. What is your favorite, and why?"

"Oooh, this is a real question," she murmured. She bit the side of her lip and rested her cheek on the back of the chair. "Rabbits," she said softly. "What's yours?"

Stark lifted his chin higher into the air. "It used to be other werewolves."

He said things that were shocking, but each revelation seemed to have something deep behind it. Other werewolves? And yet here he was, still very much alive. "And what is your favorite prey now?"

"A fox."

Chills rippled up her arms. The hunger in his eyes confused her. Did he want to kiss her or eat her? She found it hard to stand on steady ground with Stark, because he was always rocking it. As soon as she found her footing, he would say or do something that took her ankles out from under her, leaving her to search for steadier ground once again.

She kind of liked it. This conversation had her intrigued like nothing ever had before. Getting this small glimpse into the Lost Wolf's mind was revealing, intimidating, illuminating, and interesting, and had her sitting on the edge of her seat wanting to know everything—the good, the bad, and the ugly.

"You're hunting me?" she asked.

A wicked smile curved his lips. "My turn. What have you learned in the last three months?"

Another real question and not one with an easy answer. "I've learned how resilient I am. I've learned that sometimes being alone is better than feeling alone with someone. I've learned loyalty doesn't necessarily come from your blood relatives. I've learned that I can appreciate happy days and accomplishments ten times more now than I could three months ago. I've learned my reputation isn't everything. I've learned how to be a better businesswoman, and a better sister to Denver, and a better cheerleader for myself. And I've learned that maybe being hunted isn't so bad."

A strange look filled Stark's eyes. Pride? Understanding? Surprise? Perhaps a mix of all three.

"You've learned more in three months than some people learn in a lifetime." Stark leaned forward, rested his arms on his knees, and stared at the RV. "I grew up in one of these."

"In a fifth wheel?"

He nodded. "Not a nice one like this though. I lived in a ratty old bug-infested one with no constant power source. The heat ran on propane, when my old man felt like refilling the tanks. Otherwise, it was just cold." He gestured to his home. "This one is a castle."

"Where was your mom?"

"She was human."

Lyndi couldn't have been more shocked than she was in this moment. "A human?" she whispered.

"She wasn't built for the Pack I grew up in. Hell, I don't even know if my dad ever let my mom meet any of them. I don't hardly remember way back then, or maybe I just don't like to remember. People think I'm bad." Stark shook his head. "I'm a cakewalk compared to him. The Trader Pack mostly raised me. My old man would leave for weeks at a time, and the Pack would start showing up with food for me until he went broke doing whatever he was doing and returned home to work just enough to save up and disappear again. The Pack tried to find my mom when I was eleven, but said there was no trace of her. Just a missing person's report and a lot of sad kinfolks. Her family didn't even know about me, so it was easy to fall through the cracks. No one checked up unless it was the Pack. One of the pairs in that Pack tried to take me in after they couldn't find my mom. Vanna had a soft spot for me, but her mate was a cuss. He was the first wolf I fought, and back to the RV I went."

"You didn't go to school?" she whispered in horror.

Stark shook his head and twirled the orange juice bottle in his hands. "Is that enough for tonight?"

The gentle, pleading way he'd asked lanced straight through her heart. That was a lot for a wolf who kept his story locked behind chains. She could just imagine a blond, wild-haired, dirt-stained little boy spending nights alone in an old RV, waiting on his dad to come home. There were people in the world who went through great sorrows and still tried to be okay. She'd always known that, but she'd never met one until Stark. Her respect for him grew.

"It's more than enough." A man like him would run if she reacted wrong. He would make a joke and laugh it off and shut her down, but she had to touch him in some way. She had to let him know she'd heard him and it was okay, so she reached across the arms of their chairs and rested her hand in the crook of his elbow, then smiled at him. "Yesterday, you said I'm a good one. You're a good one, too."

Stark was staring at her hand where it rested on his arm. Did he feel the warmth building between them, too? "Then I tricked you well."

Mmm hmmm. A few months ago, she would've never questioned the hard shell of Stark. She would've taken him at face value, but he'd shown her too much now. She knew better. Truth be told, she liked knowing better. The world saw the mess, but that's what Stark wanted. He'd carved out a safe spot for himself by distracting people with his antics, but she wanted in. She wanted to see the real Stark.

"I grew up in this perfect house, you know? Completely opposite from you. Two parents, three sisters. I did well in school and had a lot of friends, and my problems were pretty tame. I knew what my future held from the day I was six."

"Six?"

She smiled, and already she could feel a blush in her cheeks. "On my sixth birthday, my parents bought me a hope chest. It was made of cedar, and I remember it smelled so good. It was empty when they gave it to me, but they explained that we were going to fill it with important things as I grew up, so that one day my mate could understand me without me having to say a word. They explained that I only had a certain number of years left and then I would be lucky enough to be paired up, and my life would be a happy one, just like theirs. Denver got one for her sixth birthday too, but I think she only added a pack of black hair ties to it when our parents got her in enough trouble for not filling it for her future mate. But me? My life revolved around my damn hope chest. It was all my parents talked about, and they would be so proud if I added anything. A movie stub from a theater I went to. A trophy from playing softball. A dried bouquet of lilies that my dad gave me after I was in a play. Prom pictures, and homecoming mums, collages, a T-shirt from a run I did one Saturday morning with my dad. I watched my parents with this undiluted awe, because they told me over and over that they were the pair to aspire to, and I just knew they were. There was never any holding hands, or kisses. My dad didn't pat my mom on the butt and tell her hi when he got home from work. They barely said goodbye to each other when they left the house. It was cold, but that was normal for fox pairs. So, when it came time for me to be matched up, I was well-prepared for coldness. That's what a successful pairing was about. Being friends and having kits and bettering our line. My parents had my hope chest delivered to Jake and his family before we even met. It's what helped him make the decision to choose me. Only I found out later that my dad had added something to my hope chest."

"What was it?" Stark asked in a gravelly voice.

"Money."

"Fuck." Stark shook his head and slid his hand

over hers, where it rested on his arm.

"Jake let me know that little gem when we were fighting in the first year of our pairing. He said he should've charged my father double for taking me in. I never even told my dad I know. I just got hurt and quiet, and Jake was meaner and more distant as time went on, but that's how it is, right? Perfect pairings were just friends who raised kits together. So, we tried for kits, and it didn't happen. Every month was devastating. Every month he grew colder. Meaner. And eventually, he stopped touching me altogether, and I lost who I was. But now, being out of it, I think I had never found myself in the first place, because the me I am now?" She slid her attention to Stark's face. "I would've left a long time ago for the things he said to me."

"Good girl," Stark rumbled, a darkness in his eyes that would've scared her a few months ago. Now she knew he was angry *for* her, not *at* her.

"I never had problems like you, Stark. Your story is harder. To me, it's better, because you turned out good, and that's a hard thing to do. I just wanted to tell you all of this, so you can know me better than some silly hope chest full of old memories and money. The old me doesn't matter much. The me I'm going to be does."

Stark scratched the blond scruff on his face. "You gonna show me the better you?"

"If you want. And I'll make a deal with you. Every time you tell me something real, you can have something real from me, too."

Stark swallowed hard and leaned toward her. He hesitated there, his lips inches from hers. His bright-blue eyes searched hers, and she could see it—the raw vulnerability.

Heart pounding like a drum, she eased forward and pressed her lips against his. It was short, just a three count of their warm lips touching before she disengaged and relaxed back. Short but potent. Her lips were throbbing with heat, and inside, her fox was clawing at her to kiss him again.

Stark whispered, "You're the first thing that's ever scared me."

A grin confiscated her face, and she ducked her gaze to hide her blush. "Good. Because I—"

Stark gripped the back of her neck and dragged her back to him, lips colliding with hers. Three gentle laps of his tongue before he pulled her into his lap and held her tight as he kissed the devil out of her. He didn't push, he didn't grab or make her feel trapped. He just kissed her until she understood that the raw violence of his lips was just Stark. He was a tornado that had drawn her into the eye of the storm, where it was calmer, right there in the center where the wind wasn't destructive.

Stark was beautiful instead.

TEN

Tyler, aka Gary the Bartender, had totally screwed her tonight.

He and Wanda, her most reliable server, had called in sick. Now while she could definitely cover Wanda's shift, as she'd started working here years ago as a server before she worked her way to the top, the art of drink making was definitely not a skill Lyndi possessed.

"Please order Dr Pepper on the rocks," she pleaded under her breath.

"I'll have a burlap sack," the gorgeous brunette said. Her smile was genuine and bright and ooooh, Lyndi wanted to do her drink justice for her, but what the heck was a burlap sack?

"Right. Remind me again...was that Jaaager...and...?"

The woman frowned under her baseball cap. "Vodka."

"On the rocks...?"

"I'll just have a cranberry vodka," she said.

"Oh thank God," Lyndi exhaled. "My bartender called in tonight and I'm in over my head. A cranberry vodka I can do though."

"I'm here," a deep, gravelly voice said close behind her. Stark's hand slipped to her waist and gripped it once, and Lyndi couldn't explain it, but it settled all of the panic in her chest.

"Hey!" Lyndi said, turning around. "I thought you were working late."

"I finished everything early." He gave her a blue-eyed wink. "I worked through lunch."

"And let me guess, did the jobs of four men?"

"Give me the run down. I can bartend tonight."

She must've misheard him over the noise of the busy bar. They were slammed. "What?"

He was already standing back, dragging his gaze over the two clear-door mini-fridges under the bar, the canisters of oranges, limes and cherries, and alcohol. He turned and glanced at the liquor in the cases behind him and nodded. "Memorized. I need another bottle of Jack and we are almost out of the cheap rum. Where do I get them?"

"Uuuuuh, the inventory room. Wait, you know how to bartend?"

A predatory grin drifted across his lips. "I can do a lot of things."

How was he this damn attractive, swooping in to save her once again? "Okay, hot bartender, make lots of tips tonight. I'm going to serve tables," she said, grabbing a stack of discarded menus to take back to the hostess stand.

"Hey," he called as she moved to leave. "You make lots of tips, too." He tugged at the neck of his baby blue T-shirt, and gave her a you-know-what-I'm-saying look.

Stunned, Lyndi looked down at what she was wearing. She hadn't even had a chance to take her jacket off because she'd walked into a shit show for her shift. She shrugged her coat off and pulled the V-neck of her black tank top down lower.

"Atta girl."

If it was Jake, he would've told her to keep the

jacket on and zip it up while she was at it. Stark's confidence and security with himself were very attractive traits to her. Relieved completely, Lyndi jogged over to him and tossed her jacket in a little cubby under the bar, then lifted up on her tiptoes and kissed him quick on the cheek. "Thank you."

Stark's grin turned softer, and he stood very still, leaning down slightly for her to reach him. "You're welcome."

And then she stood back and watched him work for a few seconds. The man absolutely knew how to bartend. He didn't hesitate or miss a beat; just made that lady's drink like he had made a hundred other ones before.

Stark was tall and strong, filling up every bit of space behind the bar. His boots were dirty from work, his jeans were threadbare at the knees from where he'd been leaning on a roof as he'd worked on it. He had a mud smear on his tan left arm. His strong biceps and shoulders and back pressed perfectly against the thin material of his T-shirt as he moved and worked. His smile was plastered on as he made conversation with the two new gentleman who took seats at the bar. His blond hair had been pulled back into a topknot, and the scruff on his jaw was getting a little longer. She liked the beard. Manly, sexy hunk.

He cast her a quick glance, and the smile turned into her favorite one, all crooked and real.

"Can I ask you a question before you go?" the brunette asked from her stool on the other side of the bar.

"Of course."

"Are you Lyndi Mosley?"

"I sure am," Lyndi answered, curious.

"Good." The woman pulled a manilla envelope from her oversized purse and handed it to her. "You've been served."

Baffled, Lyndi asked, "Served?"

"You can go," Stark told the woman, dumping her newly-completed drink down the sink.

Pursing her lips, the woman nodded and stood. "I'm just the messenger. I'm not sure what it's about, but I know who sent you these papers. I'm sorry." She turned and left.

The envelope was heavy in Lyndi's hands as she read the return address. Daniels and Marckam Law Firm.

Fingers fumbling, she ripped open the top and

slid the packet of papers out halfway, then read the first half of the first page in a daze.

At least it got straight to the point. Her heart dropped to the floor as she scanned the second half of the front page. This couldn't be real.

Stark set two cold beers in front of the new customers and wiped his hands on a towel as he asked, "What is it?"

"Jake is coming after me for half of my stake in this bar. He's asking for monthly payments of half the profits." She ripped her attention from the paperwork to Stark. This felt like a sword through her heart.

The wolf tipped his chin higher and huffed a humorless sound. He shook his head. "Of course he is."

"He's taking me to human courts," she said softly, so the customers couldn't hear. "We were never officially married, only paired, but he's claiming common-law marriage, and saying I bought this place when we were together. Even says he helped me buy it."

If he took half of her monthly profits, she wouldn't be able to cover her bills or afford to eat.

She wasn't rolling in the money right now. She'd just sank every penny she'd ever saved up into this place and had an all-new set of bills to show for it.

"This won't hold up," Stark assured her.

"H-how do you know?"

He leaned in closer, rested his cheek against hers, and growled a promise against her ear. "Because he won't make it to the court date. Go put that trash down and let's get through this night. We will figure that out later, when we have time."

Numbly, Lyndi nodded. In a fog of panic, she walked down the hallway and set the envelope with those damning papers in it on her desk. He was going to accomplish this. Jake always got what he wanted. He wouldn't stop until she was ruined and drained dry. That's what men like him did. It's the only way they knew how to survive. Work as little as they could and use up everyone around them until there was nothing left.

She hated him.

The swinging door to her office opened and Stark strode in, eyes full of intensity, somehow looking even bigger than he had out there. He scooped her up, wrapped her legs around his waist, and kissed every thought right out of her head.

"I can feel you panicking," he growled against her lips. "Stop. You aren't alone. He's got to get through me, and Denver, and Daylen to get to you, and good fuckin' luck. Hell, Marsden would probably eat him for fun if we took the chains off him. Settle. That snake won't get a penny of what you've worked for." Stark eased back and cupped her cheeks. "Trust me. You are in control now. He's grasping for anything. He's pathetic. You are a queen." Stark lifted her chin higher into the air with his finger. "Remember who you are."

Lyndi nodded. She probably looked like a scared bunny right now, so she composed her face. Stark was right. She wasn't the same girl she used to be. She wasn't going to roll over this time.

He jammed a finger toward the carpet. "Your territory." And then he nipped her lip and sauntered right out of her office.

The trill of fear had subsided completely, and was replaced by the growing confidence Stark was helping her discover.

She understood two new things tonight.

One: she wasn't the old Lyndi, and she could fight

Jake herself.

And just as important, number two: she wouldn't have to, because she really wasn't alone.

Lyndi blew out a steadying breath—one, and then another—and made her way out of the office to talk to the hostesses about where they needed her.

Jake could scrabble for the spoils all he wanted.

Over her cold, dead body would he get a penny.

ELEVEN

Why did it feel like a damn storm was brewing all around them?

First Tessa, and now when he finally thought they were rid of Jake, he finds a way to stress her out even more. Lyndi had worn a faraway look a dozen times tonight, and he knew that legal paperwork was weighing heavy on her mind.

Barbecued fox probably tasted awesome.

Stark finished counting his tips and made his way back to the office, where he'd seen Lyndi's purse earlier.

This was the opposite of a robbery.

Stark looked at the terrifying leather thing, sitting there, holding all of its womanly mysteries. A man worth his salt knew damn well it was dangerous messing with a woman's purse, but he had to. Lyndi wouldn't take the money he'd made unless she found it later, when it was too late to give it back. She was stubborn and independent and prideful and perfect.

Stark could hear her telling the last server goodnight out front. She would be headed back here soon, so he steeled himself and shoved the wad of cash into the side zipper compartment that was open.

He didn't know why he needed her to have the money, only that it was necessary to his existence that he feel like he took care of her in some way today. Like perhaps he could take the sting off of the hurt another man was causing.

He liked when Lyndi smiled. Everything felt right, and hopeful, when she smiled. The faraway look and solemness in her eyes tonight made his wolf want to do bad things to bad people.

He'd never been a man that fixed things before. He was a breaker. But for her? He was going to figure out a way to put her feet back on solid ground so she could make whatever progress she wanted to. Fuck, he would lay himself over mud and let her walk on him for traction if it would give her smiles. After the last few months of his wolf pining for her, he didn't care what that said about him, or what it meant. Her smiles plugged a hole in his chest that had always been bleeding, and fuck it all if it was a bad or good thing. He didn't care. He welcomed the addiction.

Like now, he swung out into the hallway, and there she was, eyes downcast and thoughtful as she pulled the hairband from her dark waves. Her cheeks were rosy from the busy night, and her full lips parted slightly. The V-neck of her skintight shirt was pulled to the side and disheveled, and her curves looked like heaven in those second-skin jeans. And when she looked up at him with those eyes the color of good whiskey, he had to stop and stare. Why? Because she pierced right through him with that addictive smile. Plug, plug, plug.

The wolf inside of him whispered the same thing he'd been saying for the last week, since Daylen had lifted the order not to see Lyndi. *Mine.*

Felt right, and to a man who hadn't felt right most of his life, he was running with this.

"Hey, Vixen." He hadn't meant for his voice to come out that growly, but she didn't seem to mind. Her cheeks went even pinker, and any remaining troubles drifted right out of her eyes. God, he would kill for her. She had no idea she had a nuke button right at her fingertips, but Lyndi was good. She was a good woman. She would never press it, and that faith in her made him feel something he'd never felt with another person before—safe. How did a man like him tell a woman like that how he felt when he didn't even know how to put into words what she did for him? What she did for his wolf?

He was going to find a way to give her little gifts every chance he got and hope she understood their meaning.

Stark would never be good at telling her he cared, but he could show her. He could figure that much out.

"Hi, Wolf," she murmured, coming to a stop right in front of him.

This was the part that had never been natural to him—touch. "I've been studying Denver and Daylen."

Surprise flitted across her features. "Oh yeah? And what have you learned?"

Stark cocked his head and leaned forward, kissed her lightly on the forehead, then eased back. Uncertain, he asked, "Did I do that right?"

Her grin stretched from ear to ear and made her

look even prettier somehow. She didn't answer him with words, just leaned in and melted into him, wrapping her arms around his waist. This was also something he was trying to learn. This was a hug. He'd tried it on Daylen once, but his Alpha had thought Stark was trying to strangle him and had punched him across the jaw. Lyndi was easier to do this with. She didn't give him bloody noses. Stark exhaled and wrapped his arms around her, careful of the pressure around her because he didn't know for certain, but he was pretty sure hugs weren't supposed to hurt or crack a girl's back.

The speakers were still playing music and a slow song was crooning. He didn't know shit about fuck when it came to dancing, but swaying her gently back and forth felt natural enough. And when she giggled and grabbed his hand—spun out and back into him smoothly—he figured he didn't even need to know how to dance. He could catch on quick with Lyndi.

She slipped her small hand against his big, callused palm, and he stared at it for a few moments as they danced. So small and perfect and soft, and such a contrast to his. They were like that...soft and rough. Usually, he wanted to fight, but with Lyndi, the wolf inside of him liked having something to protect.

"Worst night, best night," she murmured, her chin tilted up so she could see him as they swayed back and forth.

"What?" he asked, baffled.

"Name your worst night, and then your best night."

"And then you'll tell me yours?"

She nodded. "Of course. You give, I'll give."

Mmmmm. Lyndi knew what she was doing. God, she had all of his attention. He liked presents, and she was asking for a gift exchange, and okay. The first woman who had ever been interested in the real parts of him was in his arms right now.

She could have it all.

He murmured, "Don't run."

"I'm tough," she whispered.

"This is awful to revisit, but I still dream of it. I was fourteen, my dad had stopped coming around. Just...disappeared. Didn't come back to get new propane for the tanks, or drop off cans of food to last me a while. I waited. I was starving, and the wolf was keeping me alive. He hunted, and it kept me alive, but I had to stay the animal most of the time. I wasn't changing back and forth enough and my body hurt so bad. Nights I was the boy, I was freezing. Just fuckin' cold. It was winter, and snow had piled on top of the RV. One of those nights I was sleeping, the roof caved. I patched it up as best as I could but it was a mess. I woke up freezing in the middle of the night one night, and I just knew."

"Knew what?"

"My dad was dead. The bond was gone. Just...snapped."

"Oh my gosh," she whispered, pressing her cheek against his chest as she swayed with him.

"That wasn't the bad part. I didn't feel like I was supposed to. I wasn't sad that he was gone. That man was a fuckin' monster from the day he was born, and the world was better without him. I was sad that I was really going to be alone for always, because I knew I'd grow into a monster too. Who would ever understand me?" God, his guts hurt just admitting any of this. "I packed up, you know? No point in living out the last of my days in that godforsaken trailer. My dad's ghost was all over those woods and I wanted nothing to do with it. I didn't know what I was going to do. I was a kid, you know? No social skills, and I didn't understand a single thing about normal people. Or normal wolves. Talking to people was like staring at a puzzle where none of the pieces matched up. The only thing that made sense to me was the wolf. I had this old backpack, and I was standing there looking around the only house I'd ever known, and I couldn't think of anything I wanted to bring to the next life— except for this little toy cowboy my mom had gotten me for my second birthday, and a picture of her I'd hidden from my dad for all those years. That's it. That was a light backpack," he said with a chuckle. "All my belongings weighed nothing. I weighed nothing. I was skinny and hungry and numb, and I honestly don't remember how I found them."

"Who?"

"The Pack. I remembered the woman's house, the one who had tried to help me. Vanna. I don't remember trekking through the snow to get there, don't remember how many days it took. I don't remember eating or pissing or where my damn boots disappeared to. I just remember coming to standing on her front porch, barefoot, my feet purple from the cold. I couldn't stop growling, and I was shaking bad. Couldn't stop."

"You're shaking now," she murmured, hugging him tighter.

Was he? Stark lifted his hand from her back into the air, and sure enough, it was trembling like the last dead leaf on a tree in a windstorm. Fuck.

Finish it quick, the wolf told him. *Don't like this.*

Stark gripped the back of her shirt in a clenched fist to try and steady his hands. "Vanna and her mate called a Pack meeting to figure out what to do with me. There were seven males and two females in that pack. The Second to the Alpha was named Nathaniel, and he kept talking about me like I wasn't there. No one had offered me food. I was so hungry, but too proud to ask for what I needed. The wolf was begging to be let out. I didn't have control. Nathaniel kept telling the Alpha and the others that it would be a kindness to put me down. I was just like my dad. Just like my dad. Just like my dad, he kept saying. I didn't have a skill, didn't have value, didn't understand Pack dynamics because of the way my dad had raised me. Or I guess didn't raise me. Nathaniel was telling everyone I was either a lone wolf or a cull wolf. I had been sitting there—shaking, hungry—and I'd just lost the only person who would ever understand the monster in me. Nathaniel was pointing out all the bad in me and the others were nodding their heads, agreeing, and the wolf was asking to put that Second in his place, and I don't..." Stark frowned, trying hard to recall. "I don't remember exactly what happened next. Someone was shaking me. There was blood on that nice woman's walls. Screaming. The Second was laying in the corner holding his guts in while two of the other werewolves were trying to doctor him, and my mouth tasted like pennies. The Alpha wasn't strong enough. Whatever I'd done had shaken him, but I could see it in his eyes, he didn't want to put me down. He didn't know if he could. Vanna told the Alpha she would take me somewhere far away. She would take care of the problem. And she did. She told me to get into the bed of her pickup, and she drove me across two state lines, only stopping for gas, and dropped me on the doorstep of another Alpha. I was half-dead when she pulled to a stop in his territory, still frozen and starving. She told me it was the best she could do. She told me her Alpha had called, and Nathaniel would live. She wrote her phone number on a gas station receipt and shoved it into my backpack, and told me to call her if I grew up worth a damn. She was crying when she left, and I knew she didn't expect a call. She was disappointed. Felt helpless, maybe. It wasn't that my dad died, or that I was alone, or that I'd gotten into a fight that made it the worst day. It was laying in the back of that pickup, staring up at the storm clouds, the cold wind against my cheeks, another man's blood drying on my face, and knowing without a shadow of a doubt everything that Nathaniel had said was true. I was a cull wolf and not worth a damn, just like my dad."

Lyndi's eyes were rimmed with moisture when she looked up at him. "And your best day?"

Stark swallowed hard. "My best day was last week, when I sat outside of my RV and told a woman some of the awful things that built me, and told her I was scared of her, and instead of running, she let me kiss her instead."

"No cull wolves here," she murmured. "You aren't your dad. You're Stark, and you're making your own legacy. Vanna wouldn't be disappointed anymore." Her tone was filled with raw honesty as she cupped his cheeks and whispered, "You're worth a damn."

He'd never cried before. Just wasn't born with the chip inside of him that allowed him to feel that deeply, but for the first time ever, he could understand how people could. How tears could be happy. How they could mean something other than heartbreak. Stark searched her pretty eyes, and wished he had words that could make her understand how much she meant to him. Here she'd been, sitting by his heart, mending it stitch by stitch, and she didn't even realize what she was doing.

Stark spun her out and drew her back in before holding her close and swaying again.

"You catch on intimidatingly fast," she told him.

He chuckled. "Now you go. Worst day, best day."

"Okay. Worst day. I got a letter in my mailbox telling me I needed to meet with the council to dissolve my pairing and be shamed forever. I tried to call my parents, but when I told them I'd been having problems with Jake, they shut me down. Gave me advice on how to be a better mate. An acceptable one. Tips on how to keep a mate happy, because I'd been failing. That's all Jake's distance meant. So, I chickened out of telling them the council had summoned me. I just...thanked them for the advice and said I'll try harder, told them I loved them, and hung up the phone. Never in my life had I felt so alone. I walked out the door the morning of the meeting knowing it would be a bad day, and it was a hard one. A lot of emotions. A lot of feeling like a failure, and like I'd made all the wrong decisions to get myself into a hole that deep."

Stark nodded. "And your best?"

"Best day. I got a letter in my mailbox telling me I needed to meet with the council..."

Stark frowned and eased back to look her in the face as she finished.

"...and a man I barely knew swept in and made sure I didn't do that alone. And everything I'd been feeling was turned upside down. Instead of being defeated, I started accepting things faster, and turning around my life in a way I would've never been brave enough to do if that man hadn't stomped through that door behind me and made sure I held my head up high as those people tried to tear me down. I learned more in that day than I have any other day on this earth. It turned out to be the best day for me, and also the most important." She gave a lopsided grin. "And then the sexy man disappeared for three months and completely confused me."

He belted out a single laugh. "I was ordered to!

Daylen wasn't messing around. In his defense though, I did use you every time I wanted to get under his and Denver's skin."

"What do you mean?"

"Every time they annoyed me, I would tell them I was going to bang Denver's sister."

Lyndi tossed her head back and laughed. "Miscreant."

"I don't know what that insult means, but it's probably true."

"So are you?" she asked, a wicked glint he'd never seen before in her eyes.

"Am I what?"

"Gonna bang Denver's sister?"

Truth be told, he'd never wanted a woman so badly before.

Truth be told, he'd tried to take it slowly because he wanted something deeper with Lyndi.

Truth be told, yeah, if she said go, he was going to get her addicted to him so she'd never want to leave him.

She was teasing him, but this little vixen didn't know what she was asking for.

When the time came, Stark was going to enjoy

every second of teaching her.

TWELVE

Stark was having trouble looking away from her.

Lyndi was sleeping in his bed tonight, on her side, the soft blue moonlight filtering through his open window. The breeze was cold tonight, and while he had to sleep with a window open so his wolf wouldn't feel trapped, he had obsessed all night over whether Lyndi was too cold or not.

Maybe he should get her another blanket.

No. Stop. You've already piled two on top of her and she kicked out of them.

Hungrily, he drank in the length of her long leg draped over the covers. It had been so hard to stay off her last night. They'd gotten back here late after she'd closed up Zaps, and stayed up talking until she'd fallen asleep on his couch. He'd carried her in here, and hadn't been able to sleep at all.

Unable to help himself, he brushed his fingertips up the side of her thigh. So silky smooth. She smiled in her sleep and wiggled closer. To him. Lyndi felt safe here, with him. His mind had been blown thirty times in the last week.

Stark needed to go. He had plans. He had things he needed to accomplish. Things Lyndi couldn't know about until after they were done, because she was a good person who worried Stark would go too far.

She had no idea how far he could go, but it was kind of cute watching her worry over him. Someday she would figure out what he was capable of, but not today. Not tonight. She wasn't addicted to him enough yet. Too soon.

The wolf growled softly in his chest again, and he swallowed it down. *Don't wake her.*

I want to see her eyes. Are they gold, like her fox's, when she wakes up?

Stark gritted his teeth and stood. He needed to leave before wolf convinced him waking Lyndi up in the middle of the night was a good idea.

Lyndi slipped her hand into his and squeezed,

halting him from leaving.

Gold. Her eyes were gold when she woke up.

"Where are you going?" she whispered.

Stark shook his head in denial. She couldn't know about the dark deeds he had planned.

Lyndi studied his face in the moonlit room for a few seconds, and then tugged his hand, lifted up the edge of the covers invitingly. She was only wearing one of his old tank tops, and the fabric had hiked up her creamy thigh. Every soft inch of her skin from her hips down was bathed in the dim light. "Come put me back to sleep before you go."

His dick throbbed with wanting. No point in trying to deny her. He couldn't even if he tried. She could have anything she wanted.

Stark pushed his gray sweatpants down his hips and slid under the covers with her, rolled on top of her and settled between her thighs. One nip on the neck and she reacted, arching her head back and releasing a soft growl that dredged chills of desire all the way up his spine.

Stark dragged his fingertips down her outer thigh until he reached the back of her knee, and as he bent her leg deeper, he pushed into her, slow and deep.

Already wet for him. Good little vixen. Fuuuuuuck she felt tight around him. Stark rolled his eyes closed and buried his face against the side of her neck as he eased back, then pushed in again.

Her nails were already on his back, gripping as he moved inside of her. Every gasp she made, every sound, pushed him to slow it down. Sweet torture for both of them. So slick, and the way she gripped his cock with her body...*fuck.*

Stark kept the pace smooth and calculated, until she was crying out on every stroke. He only paused when she cried out his name and came for him. He wanted to feel her pulsing. Deep again. And again. It felt so good, like nothing ever had before. There was no stopping now, he was too close, and she was moaning his name mindlessly now. Everything about this woman turned him on. Stark gripped the back of her neck and drove into her harder, faster. Felt good. Felt like everything.

I love you I love you I love you...

Lyndi's whispered words drifted through the bond they had begun building, filling his mind with something he'd never felt before. It was the greatest drug.

Love? Love. Had he ever heard that word before? He couldn't recall a single time that was aimed at him.

He didn't know how to say those words back. They weren't part of his vocabulary, but he wanted her to know how important she was.

Easing back to look at her face, Stark growled out a question he hoped to God she had an answer for. "Am I yours?"

Lyndi eased her bright-gold eyes open and looked up at him. She didn't answer him with words. Instead, she tilted her head to the side and exposed her throat, and holy shit, he would never forget the arch of her neck as she told his wolf everything he needed to know.

Stark could already feel his canines elongating, could feel the animal pushing. Everything was intense—her gripping his dick with her body, the wolf preparing to do something he swore to never do.

Stark bucked deep into her and the pressure was there. Fuck, he was going to come. God, he wanted to fill her, he wanted her smelling like him always. Wanted her to walk around with his cum inside of her every day for the rest of her life and God...dammit...

His dick throbbed hard inside of her, and he gave in to the wolf. He leaned down and sank his teeth into the space where her neck met her shoulder.

She gasped, but it wasn't a pained sound. As he came, she arched against the mattress and her body clenched around him. Fuck, she was coming with him and he couldn't even think straight with the wolf howling in his head, the throbbing of his cock, and the taste of her blood in his mouth.

He pushed into her slower, because she deserved for him to drag out her orgasm. She deserved to feel every pulse of that release. She deserved everything.

Chest heaving, Stark forced himself away from the claiming mark he'd just made on her. He sat back on his bent knees and held her knees open wide with his hands. He didn't care what it said about him. The monster inside of him loved the view of her legs spread wide and his cum dripping out of her.

He didn't do labels. Not until now, but the possessive wolf inside of him was in full control of his words now. "You're mine, Lyndi." He leaned over her, locking an arm by her face as she stared up at him with hooded, sated eyes. Stark slid two fingers into her just to feel her again, and she exhaled, spread her knees farther apart. Sexy vixen, so pliable under his touch. So reactive. So damn sexy.

Lowering down to his elbow so he could nip her ear, he fingered her slowly. She was high as a kite right now from what he was doing to her body—he could tell. One more wouldn't hurt before he left. One more to put her back to sleep. He pushed his fingers deeper into her and she groaned softly as she ran her fingers up to his still pulled-back hair. She tugged at the band he'd used to tie it back, and she released his hair. The length of it fell to the side, and she dragged her nails through it. "When people ask if I'm taken, I'll tell them I belong to you," she whispered.

A moan racked his body, and he fingered her faster. "You can tell them I belong to you."

Her breaths were coming in pants now, and she was moving her hips with the pace he set with his fingers.

Lyndi placed her hand on his throat and squeezed gently, looked him deep in the eyes and whispered, "Stark Wulfson belongs to me."

He was rock hard again in an instant. Stark slid his wet fingers out of her and kissed her as he plunged his cock back into her. This wasn't soft and slow. This was raw and hard. This was seeing how deep he could fill her. It was fucking her like the demon he was—her hand on the headboard, her cries ripping out of her throat until they shattered together again.

He ran his tongue across the claiming mark, cleaning her as he stayed hovered over her, dick throbbing inside of her again, matching her slowing release. Good girl, knowing how to push his body. Good girl for taking his dick so well.

He rewarded her by worshipping her body. He explored every sensitive inch of her skin, kissed down her arms, down her belly and back to her throat. *Mine, mine, mine*, the wolf chanted.

God, it was dangerous to give the monster something to possess. Did she realize what she'd allowed him to do? Lyndi had allowed a claiming mark that would tether his wolf to her for eternity. She'd chosen a monster and allowed a monster to choose her back. She had the fealty of the wolf now, and all the darkness that would encompass. Perhaps her good would rub off on the animal...or perhaps not.

Either way, Lyndi was safe for always now,

because without a shadow of a doubt, Stark knew he would bleed dry every person who aimed at her, just to ensure her happiness.

A good man would protect the world.

A bad man would burn the world to the ground to protect one woman.

Stark wasn't a good man.

He kissed her forehead, slid out from under the covers, and pulled on the jeans that he'd draped over the small storage bench in his bedroom.

"Where are you going?" Lyndi asked in a sleepy voice.

Stark buttoned up the jeans and knelt by the bed, pulled her small hand to his lips and let a kiss linger there. *Queen.* "To get your hope chest back. That belongs to me now."

THIRTEEN

To get her hope chest back?

Lyndi sat straight up. "Jake still has it."

"I know," Stark rumbled, pulling a T-shirt over his chiseled torso.

Lyndi swallowed hard. "Can I come too?"

Stark slid her a bright blue-eyed look over his shoulder. "You won't be able to change what happens."

And she understood. He was really saying 'you won't be able to change me, or how I have to handle the things I feel I need to handle.'

Perhaps she didn't have a right to change that part of him. Perhaps that was part of what she loved about him—that black and white view of the world. If something struck him as wrong, Stark corrected it.

He was intimidating, and dangerous, and sexy. A layer of comfort slid over her shoulders that she was under the wing of his protection and not outside of it.

"I'll get dressed," she murmured.

After a loaded few moments, Stark nodded his head. The change in him was there already, in the color of his eyes, in the somberness there. He was the hunter now.

She dressed as fast as she could, brushed her teeth, and ran a brush through her hair before she pulled it back to the nape of her neck. At the front door, Stark stood with an oversized flannel, open for her to slip into. She did. It smelled like fur and forest and the cologne he wore, and Lyndi pulled it tighter around her shoulders as she followed him out of the RV and into the darkness. The clock in the truck read 5:15, and the first gray light of dawn was just peeking over the horizon as they made their way out of Daylen's territory and down to the main road.

Stark's hair was still down from when she'd pulled the band out of it earlier, and it was flipped over to the other side of his face, giving her the perfect view of the buzzed side of his head and sharp features. He didn't turn up the music, but that was okay. She kind of liked the silence in the moments before dawn with him. It felt like they were the only ones in the world who were awake.

He slid his hand across the top of her thigh, and when she smiled over at him, he cupped her neck, right above where he'd given her the claiming mark. It burned, but she didn't mind the pain. It was a reminder of what he'd done. Foxes didn't do claiming marks, but some wolves did if they followed the old ways. Denver had told her about it before. Stark's wolf apparently followed the traditional werewolf ways. She didn't know why, but it made her respect him more. Made her like him and appreciate him more. He was so different from anyone she'd ever met before, and with every revelation, every layer exposed, she was drawn in closer. She was more interested in what made a man like Stark tick.

"Killing Jake won't fix things for me," she murmured in the silence of the cab.

He stared straight ahead at the road illuminated by his headlights, so she tried again. "Daylen will have to put you down if anyone finds out you ended him, and I'll be left alone to deal with the council, who will rain hell down on my life, and my family's lives."

"Your family doesn't understand loyalty."

"Maybe not, but I have to believe they wouldn't join the mob."

"You want a relationship with them," he murmured.

It wasn't a question, but she nodded her answer anyway. "There is nothing quite like the feeling of your parents being proud of you when you are succeeding."

"You're succeeding now," he said, a slight frown marring his features.

"I see that, and you see that, but they don't know how to see it. Not yet. Maybe someday they will though, after enough time has passed."

"You want to keep your family," he murmured softly.

She frowned, confused.

He dragged his gaze to her. "You should have everything you want."

What she wanted and what would actually happen were two entirely separate things. She was mated to a werewolf, and not just any werewolf—the Lost Wolf. There would be no acceptance. She'd given up on that the day she'd been shunned by the council and deemed a cull fox. That shame would haunt generations of Mosleys. And her sister pairing up with Daylen didn't help. Her parents probably felt like they were on an island with sharks all around them, and she understood. They were undoubtedly the talk of all fox shifters right now. They had barely spoken to her over the last three months, but that didn't change the little corner of Lyndi's heart that remembered all the good things about growing up with them.

"You are careful with cutting loyalty ties," Stark observed.

"Yes. It takes a lot for me to quit on a person."

The corner of Stark's lip quirked up. "Sometimes I think you were born to the wrong clan."

"What do you mean?"

He cast her a quick glance, then back to the road as he turned onto the driveway of Jake's family home. "You were supposed to be a werewolf instead. You would've been an Omega."

"The lowest ranking member in a wolf pack?" she asked with a giggle. "Thanks."

"Not the lowest ranking like you understand it,"

153

he said. "Omegas bring peace to bonds. They can settle entire packs. Vanna was an Omega. She was a fixer. I haven't met another one since. You would've been a peacemaker. You would've attracted every wolf within three states if anyone would've ever figured out you were an Omega. I thought you were submissive when I first met you. I pitied you. I thought the world probably chewed you up and spat you out, but then I watched you stand up to Tessa. You aren't submissive at all. You are careful before you react, and you cause as little pain in this world as you can. Being soft toward people who have been kind to you at a point in time isn't a weakness. It's a strength. It's easier to throw your middle fingers up at the people who make mistakes around you, but you don't do that. You take time to try and understand them instead. I've never been able to do that. It wouldn't even cross my mind to try and understand people's reasoning for anything. They are good or bad to me, and the bad are taught a lesson. I am Karma. You are the voice of reason that asks, 'but why?'. If you could slip into the skin of a wolf, you would be an Omega."

He stopped in the circular driveway of Jake's

family home, put the truck into park, and stared at the front door with frost in his glare. "Tell me what to do."

Inside the house, a light flickered on. "Wait by the truck. I will get you your hope chest."

A soft growl rattled Stark's throat. "You can't protect him forever."

"Who says I'm protecting Jake?" she asked. "He can burn." She pushed open the door. "I'm protecting you." Lyndi gave him a wink. "I don't want you choking on his carcass."

She caught his wicked smile just before she turned to see Jake at the front door, his parents and four brothers behind him.

"You're outnumbered," Jake said.

"Yet it's still not a fair fight," Stark said from where he leaned on the front of his truck behind her. "For you."

"What do you want?" Jake demanded. He looked puffy and tired.

"I want my hope chest back. It doesn't belong to you anymore."

Jake slid a gold-eyed glare to Stark and back to her. "You fuck werewolves now?" he spat out.

The old Lyndi would've gone quiet and let shame heat her cheeks. She wasn't that girl anymore, though. "Yeah, I needed an upgrade from your trash dick."

Stark snorted behind her.

"I'm not giving back the money your dad paid me for you," he gritted out. "I earned that."

"I don't want the money. I just want the chest. It doesn't belong to you anymore." She twitched her head. "It belongs to him. I'm the nice one. I'm asking politely. Keep standing there arguing with me and I'll let the wolf have you."

She could feel Stark's presence grow, and Jake's eyes went wide. She knew Stark had stood to his full height and was standing right at her back now.

"Be a good boy and go retrieve it for us," Stark rumbled in a voice that wasn't even slightly human. God, the air felt like cement in her lungs, and she struggled to keep her composure under the weight of Stark's dominance. Ooooh, clever man. He kept this part hidden from the world, and she had a feeling this wasn't all of it. If his fingertips hadn't put pressure on the low of her back at that exact moment and released the heaviness from her lungs, she would've been as scared as Jake's family looked.

Without another word, Jake and his brothers disappeared inside, and his father stepped out onto the porch. "You have been such a disappointment," he told her. "This isn't over."

"Oh, I got your little papers," she said. "I figured you were the one paying for the lawyers, because what does your son have? He's living with mommy and daddy, trying to steal money from the woman he destroyed so he can convince himself, and you, that he isn't worthless." She gave an empty smile. "You know better though, don't you? *You* have been such a disappointment," she told him, reciting his words.

Jake's mom dropped her gaze and melted back inside, and without another word, Jake's father followed.

Jake and his youngest brother, Earnest, brought the chest out and set it just beyond the porch. The look in Jake's eyes was pure fury as he stared at Lyndi. In a flash, he lifted his boot high into the air to slam it down onto the chest, but Stark appeared out of thin air, took his bent leg, and slammed Jake to the ground. He hit him just once...one swing of his stone fist and Jake's face was rearranged. He was rolling from side to side, howling in pain, holding his bleeding nose as Stark stood over him, fists clenched at his side.

Zero percent surprised, Lyndi told the idiot, "I tried to warn you."

Stark twisted around to look at her. "I really can't kill this motherfucker?"

"Is he worth it?"

"Yes!" he said in an exasperated tone.

Lyndi laughed, but coughed to try and cover it. At least he was honest.

Stark lurched at him, bluffing, and Jake screamed and curled in on himself. Stark picked up the chest like it weighed nothing at all and muttered, "I guess we'll see you in human courts, you burning bag of dogshit. Have your mommy pray for your soul if you actually win a single penny of Lyndi's money. Listen to the honesty in my voice when I swear to you, I will never stop hunting you." A crack of power rippled through the air like a lightning strike. Whooo, the last of his words burned like fire against her ears.

Stark was harboring a very potent animal, and she thought she was only seeing the beginning of what he could do. She blinked hard and shook her head, trying to recover from the shock of Stark's cobra-strike speed and capability for remorseless violence.

Monster. Her monster.

Feeling lighter, she hopped up in the passenger side of Stark's truck while he secured the chest in the back with bungee cords. And by the time Stark climbed behind the wheel, she had tracked down the perfect song on her phone to blare through the speakers.

And then she and Stark left Jake's family territory blaring "Highway to Hell", and no one could wipe the slowly-growing grin off her face if they tried.

Stark was pissed. Fury vibrated off him in waves, but by the second verse of the song, the snarl on his lips had softened and his eyes were a somewhat-normal color of blue. She even caught him tapping his finger against the wheel, but his gaze stayed faraway and focused on something internal.

He pulled into a gas station, but he still had half a tank. "Ooooh," she teased. "You're one of those people."

"What people?"

"There are two types of people. The ones who fill

up their tank at half empty, and the ones how know exactly how long they can go until they coast into a gas station on fumes."

"Let me guess. You are a fumes kinda girl."

"Yep."

He lifted her hand to his lips and kissed her skin there, then bit her gently, a wicked glint in his eyes. "I'm a fumes kinda guy. I'm just here for the breakfast burritos."

"Oh." She frowned. "Gas stations have breakfast burritos?"

"This one does. You are about to have your mind blown. I need food. The wolf has been pushing to come out since we pulled up to that house. It's not..." His words faded away and he stared out the front window.

"It's not what?"

"It's not easy to pull the wolf off a fight."

Lyndi cupped her hands around the back of his neck and angled his face to hers. Searching his eyes, she told him, "You did good."

The tightness that had etched right into the corners of his eyes faded away, and the growl that had been softly rattling his chest since they'd left the

RV quieted.

"I found the money you shoved in the side of my purse, turd. You didn't have to do that. Breakfast burritos are my treat."

"Sorry, Scooter. Not this time. I need to buy these." He gave her a wink and shoved his door open, then hopped out before she could react to the random nickname.

Surprised, she giggled and grabbed her purse, then hopped out of his truck too. She was still warm and enveloped in his huge flannel. He was waiting for her and as soon as she reached him, he pulled the oversized warm shirt tighter around her, then dragged her to him and kissed her quick. He draped his heavy, powerful arm over her shoulders, and such a feeling of safety washed over her. It was dawn, and there was only one other car in the parking lot. Stark's attention stayed on the blue Bronco that was parked in the shadows over by the dumpster for a couple of moments before he opened the door for her. Lyndi didn't recognize it, but it looked like no one was in it.

It must've belonged to the cashier inside, who offered them a friendly wave and a, "Good morning."

Stark was probably always like this, observing everything around him. She liked that. It freed her up to loosen up and just be her happy little self. Stark created safe spots for her, and it was something she appreciated more and more.

The breakfast burritos were custom orders in a little cafeteria-style setup along the back wall. The woman who filled their orders was very kind and genuine, and Stark was nice and relaxed as he ordered way too many burritos for them to ever eat in one sitting.

"You really feel like we need fifteen breakfast burritos?" she asked after he paid and opened the exit for her.

"It's not all for us." Stark's eyes darted to the shadows of the parking lot again, but the Bronco was gone. A couple of cars had pulled up to the gas pumps but he didn't pay them any mind. Huh.

"Who was that?" she asked because that old saying about curiosity killing the cat also applied to fox shifters.

"Oh, just a terrible coincidence." But his tone was off. He was fibbing, but she didn't understand which word had tripped him up—terrible or coincidence.

"Fine, keep your secrets," she muttered, grabbing the giant paper bag of food from his hands. "I will drown my sorrows in salsa verde."

"You like the green sauce, and I like the red. How can we ever expect this to work out?"

The crackle of the paper on her burrito as she shredded through the top filled the cab of the truck. "What is the 'this' in that question? Hmm?" she said around a bite. "You don't like labels, remember?"

His eyes sparked with hunger and he leaned in fast, latched his teeth gently onto her earlobe, and released her. "You know what you are," Stark growled against her ear.

She went still, stunned, as fireworks went off in her chest. Inside of her, the fox was practically purring with devotion.

Stark slid his hand slowly down the inside of her leg, and she melted into him. "You could make me do anything. If you said go jump off a cliff, I would say, 'cool, do you want a soda before I go?'"

Stark laughed and eased back. "If you go jumping off any cliffs, I'll never bone you again."

She took another bite of burrito and rolled her eyes closed in ecstasy. She'd just gotten to the cheese and eggs and bacon part. "How did I not know this existed in this town until now?"

"Every roofer and construction worker for twenty miles around knows about this place. It's the best breakfast in three counties that you can get at the crack of dawn."

Lyndi poured a drizzle of red hot sauce on the burrito and offered it to Stark, who took a bite without hesitation, like they'd done it a hundred times before. The next bite was hers, with green sauce, as he pulled out of the parking lot. "Are the others for your work crew?" she asked.

"Nope. They're for your momma."

Lyndi snorted. "Okay, and on to the 'your momma' jokes."

"No, seriously. They're for your parents. You're going to introduce me to them."

The bite of burrito she was chewing nearly fell out of her mouth. "Come again?"

He didn't elaborate, just took a right on Cleffield Drive, which was the exact right way to her parents' house. "How do you know where they live?"

"Maybe I visited there before."

Lyndi turned her body toward him and curled her

knees up. "Spill it, mister. Why would you have gone to my parents?"

Stark clenched his jaw and shook his head slightly.

She didn't want him to shut down though. She wanted him to tell her everything. She wanted to know him. To really know him.

"Please," she whispered.

He sighed and turned onto Mayfield Avenue, then straight into her parents' driveway. Their lights were all on, as she knew they would be. Her parents woke before the sun every day. They always had. Early bird gets the worm, and all. Stark stared out the front windshield, his elbow resting on the window beside him, chewing on the corner of his thumbnail. "I missed you."

Lyndi's heart was warm in her chest, glugging lava through her veins. She pulled her phone from the cupholder and opened up the picture Denver had sent. The one where Stark was sitting next to her fox, staring at her like she was all he could see.

Gingerly, he took the phone from her and studied the picture. Swallowing audibly, he handed it back to her and nodded. "Daylen said to stay away from you, but I could come here when you weren't around. He shrugged. I was hurt. I'd gone after Tessa. Chasing an Alpha out of a territory takes its toll." His eyes looked a hundred years old right now. "I was having trouble healing, and I wasn't resting because I needed to hunt Jake, but when I came here, sometimes it felt like I was kind of close to you, and I felt..."

"Better?"

"Better. It's never been like that. People make me want to crawl out of my own skin when they are too close for too long. You are the only person who hurts me if you're away too long. Terrifying creature."

Lyndi slipped her hand into his and squeezed. "I feel better around you, too. I think that's how this is supposed to be."

His sharp features softened with his smile. He twitched his chin toward the house. "Let's go."

"Stark!" she said, panic fluttering in her stomach. "Whatever happens in there, it doesn't change you and me."

He angled his face and dipped his gaze to her lips. "You deserve to have what you want."

Silly boy. Didn't he see? What she wanted was him.

He slid out of the truck and unloaded the hope chest out of the bed of the truck. She didn't understand, but he was quiet and looked thoughtful, so she grabbed the paper bag of burritos and her purse and walked beside him as he carried the heavy cedar chest up to the front door.

Dad met them there, opened the door with a spark of anger in his eyes. *Here we go.*

"Hi, Dad."

His jaw clenched, and instead of greeting her back, he leveled Stark with a look that could chill an iceberg. "I know who you are. Why did you bring that back here?"

Stark set it down and offered his hand for a shake. "Mr. Mosley, you won't shake my hand right now, but I'm going to offer it. I'm going to keep offering it and hope that someday you will look past whatever you've heard of me, and get to know me."

Dad crossed his arms and refused the shake. Stark nodded and let his hand fall to his side. "Can we come in? Lyndi had some things she wants to talk to you about."

"I think it's best you stay out here," he said to Stark.

"Todd," her mother whispered from just behind him. Lyndi could see her hand on his arm, and when she peeked around him, her eyes were puffy, as if she'd been crying.

Her father cut her off. "I don't want to hear it. I've been—"

"Enough," Lyndi snapped. "I know you hate me. I know you hate what happened and you hate the shame on our family, and you think I could've somehow stopped it. And maybe I could've." Her eyes burned already. "Maybe I could've been a little more broken, and learned to not speak or think for myself. Maybe I could've learned to live with Jake doing whatever he wanted, and learned to live with a thousand rules on me. Maybe with enough time I could've gotten used to be treated like I was nothing." She shrugged up her shoulders, and the first tears fell to her cheeks. "I failed at breaking, Dad."

Stark's fingertips went to her back and massaged gentle circles as she sniffed and straightened her spine. "I tried it your way. I tried really hard, and it wasn't for me. Your way worked for you, and I had this great childhood, but my story is different." She dashed her knuckles across her wet cheeks. "Denver's story is different. Stark's story…it's different. But I hope that someday you see that different doesn't mean wrong. It just means different. I love you both very much, and I miss you. I miss the way you looked at me, like I was doing all right, but I also understand that everything has changed." She huffed a sigh and bumped Stark's shoulder, smiled shakily up at him. "It's still changing." She handed her dad the bag of burritos. "Stark listened to me when I said I love you, and he wants me to be able to keep you. We brought you breakfast."

Dad's arms stayed crossed, but Mom stepped around him and took the offering from her. "Come on inside," she said softly.

Lyndi followed her mom, but Stark stayed where he was, looking like a giant Viking on the front stoop. Dad was staring him down, but if Stark was riled up, he wouldn't have been able to. Stark had his chin tilted down, and the snarl in his chest didn't exist right now.

"You didn't answer my question," Dad said. "Why did you bring that back here?"

"The hope chest is mine and Lyndi's now. We will fill it together with new memories. She doesn't want the things from her past, but I imagine if I had a mother or a father who had been worth anything, perhaps they would've wanted my keepsakes. Perhaps you want Lyndi's."

Lyndi held her breath through the next few tense seconds, but finally, Dad's shoulders relaxed and he stepped out of Stark's way.

With a slight nod, Stark ducked under the doorframe and sauntered at Lyndi's side until they reached the kitchen table, where her mother was setting out plates and glasses of orange juice.

And over the next two hours, as she watched Stark's composure while he was grilled by her dad, she fell in love a little harder. Watching him soften her parents, be understanding, shake off tension, and put her at ease when she began shaking her leg in nervous habit when things were uncomfortable, she found herself grateful. Stark already had her. He didn't have to do this dance with her parents. He was here because he wanted to fix something in her life that was broken.

And that's how this was supposed to be, right? If you were lucky, you found someone who cared enough to find the glue for the shattered pieces.

Someone strong enough to hold them together while the jagged edges dried.

She'd found him. Lyndi knew it without a shadow of a doubt. He'd gone after Tessa for her, gone after Jake for her, and now here he was in the early morning hours, talking at her parents' dinner table without a trace of fear or awkwardness.

How could her parents not be impressed? Werewolf or not, Lost Wolf or not, Stark answered every question with confidence and honesty. All of his answers led back to Lyndi, and how she would be protected and coveted. He included her. Asked her how she felt about what they were talking about. Time and time again, he made space for her to have her say.

It was becoming increasingly clear that Stark wasn't going to allow her to be invisible ever again.

FOURTEEN

Stark hated this part.

He'd told Lyndi he could do a lot of things well before, and he hadn't been lying. No one really knew what he could do, and he liked that. He liked keeping his cards close to his chest. Lyndi would figure him out someday, and that part, he didn't mind. But the rest of the Pack? It was best if they just thought he was a screwup with a hairpin-trigger temper.

He'd just gotten home from work, knowing what he had to do, but God he dreaded it. Tessa was gnarly to tangle with, and she left him drained. Bright side? He was putting a drain on her too.

Her fuckin' Bronco had been parked at the gas station, and that meant she was back in town, and he knew exactly why.

He'd taken her hunt away from her, and Tessa wasn't okay anymore. The loss of Vager had destroyed any good she'd had in her before, and the subsequent shunning from Daylen's pack had turned her heart the color of tar. And that right there was one of Stark's talents. He could see black hearts. No...he could feel them. Sense them. He recognized them, because for a long time, one of them had beat inside of his own chest.

Poison.

He could manipulate poison, and Tessa was a quick shot of cyanide.

She was close. The old sickened bonds she'd kept with this pack pulsed with darkness as Stark closed his eyes and reached for it in his mind. There were good bonds. Strong ones. Healthy ones glowing white, pulsing with happiness. Marsden was at his home, working on his Jeep. Daylen was inside his house talking on the phone with Denver, who was on her lunch break at her job. Daylen had the day off. Stark brushed that bond with his mind a little too hard. He couldn't help it. Daylen was so happy talking to his mate, that energy latched onto him and yanked him in.

Daylen's attention snapped to the bond. *What are you doing?*

Stark flinched away and kept searching. A soft-pink bond conjured a smile, and he almost lost where he was. Lyndi. He wasn't here for this, but he stretched for her bond. It was stronger than it had been yesterday, and he knew what that meant. She was tethering herself to him. She cared about him. She cared. About him. Soft murmured words drifted from the bond, and he couldn't make them out at first. Closer, closer...

Lyndi was singing to herself, humming a song he couldn't quite decipher. Her voice was so pretty, it called him in closer. Little siren. Her bond was flooded with contentment. He didn't have time for this, but he couldn't help it...he stayed. She was refilling napkin canisters at the bar. There were only a few customers. Beside the stack of napkins were flyers advertising Denver singing there on Saturday night. She was thinking about him. Thinking about how handsome he was, thinking about the things he'd said to her parents, thinking about how lucky she felt to have found him. He shouldn't be here. These were her private thoughts, but oh God, it was addictive to see himself through her eyes. Did he really look like that? Did his smile really stretch that big around her? He'd always been at war with the man he saw in the mirror, but the reflection in Lyndi's mind changed everything. She saw the good in him.

Daylen was coming. Stark's sensitive ears picked up the open and close of Daylen's house door, and his heavy boot-steps outside, coming closer.

Don't lose focus. Almost there, the wolf whispered.

Daylen opened the door to his RV, and Stark winced but didn't open his eyes. He held a finger up to his lips.

He could hear the question through Daylen's bond. The confusion. To his Alpha's credit though, he could've slammed all those bonds closed on Stark, and he didn't. He sat on the loveseat near the couch where Stark was, and stilled.

Trust, Daylen murmured through the bond.
Good Alpha.

Behind Lyndi's pink bond was the hidden one. Tessa was smart to hide it there, because it was hard for any of them to get to it. The bond was jagged and thin, and a cloud of black fog drifted from it. It crackled with sparks as he drew closer. He reached for it and strangled the bond with his power.

"Close the bonds," he murmured to Daylen. "Protect them."

Dear God, let the Alpha be smart enough to know what he meant.

Behind him, Stark could feel the Pack bonds squeezing closed. Marsden and Denver all but disappeared. Daylen stayed open, and so did Lyndi.

I'm not her Alpha, Daylen whispered across his bond. *I can't close her off.*

Shit. He didn't want Lyndi to feel what he was about to do. Could he close her off?

Stark kept his grip on the black bond and aimed at the pink one. A cold sweat broke out across his forehead as he concentrated on thinning Lyndi's bond. It was so happy, so distracting. So addictive. Nothing in him wanted to close off the sensations of joy and care, but Lyndi would be scared if she saw this. Stark clenched his fists. This was taking too long. When he fucked with bonds, he only had so long before he was drained. He'd learned that from experience, but the effort was worth it. This was for Lyndi.

The pink bond thinned...thinned...

Jesus, Daylen whispered. *What are you?*

Stark ignored him, slammed Lyndi's bond closed, and turned to the dark bond. Tendrils of power stretched out from him to the bond as he pulsed exactly what he needed to into it.

"I have to go," Stark told Lyndi. "It'll just be a couple of days."

"I don't understand why you have to do this," Lyndi said low. "Why can't Daylen do it himself?"

"Because he has to stay in this territory, at least for a while. Hey," Stark said, drawing closer to her. He ran a fingertip down her soft cheek. "I'll be back before you know it, and hopefully with some new wolves for the Pack. With Tessa building up, we need numbers. Daylen wants me to meet them and decide on who we allow here. He's a dick, but I actually agree with him. We have too much to protect to be this low on numbers. It's one thing if it's just me and Marsden and Daylen going down, but you and Denver need protection. This is the way to do it. We're weak. Three wolves is not enough, and we haven't built up our bonds well enough. I can't even trust Marsden to

fucking back us up if Tessa came here with her new Pack. We need this, Lyndi."

She fiddled with the flyers for Saturday night, her eyes downcast.

"Hey," he murmured, hooking a finger under her chin to drag those pretty amber eyes back up to him. "You don't have to be scared. Daylen will be around if you need anything, and so will Marsden. You can ask Denver to stay with you the nights I'm gone."

"I just..." she looked tortured, and gripped his shirt in her clenched fists. "I have this awful feeling, Stark."

"That's just fear talking, Lyndi. You're stronger than that now."

"When do you leave?"

"Tomorrow morning."

She inhaled sharply. "So soon. When will you be home?"

"Three days." He dragged her against his chest and held her close. "Three little days and I'll be back here annoying the shit out of Daylen and Marsden again."

She let off a pretty little giggle. "Three days. I'll ask Denver to stay with me. That would actually make me feel better. We could use some girl time."

"Good." He eased her back to arm's length. "Now

quit being such a little scaredy-cat. I'm building you an army. You're safe."

Daylen sat on the couch silently, eyes trained on Stark, his elbows on his knees, hands clasped between them.

"Welcome to the shit show," Stark ground out weakly.

"You're still in there, aren't you?" Daylen's voice was hoarse, like the work Stark had done had taken a toll on him as well.

With a grunt, Stark rested his head back on the couch. He didn't have enough strength to even clench his fists right now. "In Tessa's head, I'm driving back here. She hates the song I'm listening to. I can tell. She's getting tired of watching me. She's making plans."

"You just gave her bait, didn't you?" Daylen asked softly.

Sweat dripped down Stark's face as he nodded slightly.

"Fuck," Daylen murmured as he pulled his clenched hands in front of his mouth and stared out the window of Stark's RV.

Tessa was drifting off. She was making calls now, calling in her new Pack. All he had to do now was close off his bond to the Pack, and Tessa wouldn't feel what he was doing. That was easy. He was good at shutting down from all the years of practice.

The moment Stark strangled his bond, Daylen flinched in pain, and then dragged his lightened gaze to Stark. "Why didn't you fight for it?"

"Fight for what?" Stark asked in a strained voice.

"Alpha. That's what you are, right? You're Lyndi's Alpha. You dragged her into this Pack without me even creating that bond. You can manipulate bonds better than anyone I've ever seen, besides Tessa. Why didn't you fight for it?"

"Fuck being Alpha," Stark muttered. "I would be shit at it and you know it. Just because a man is born strong doesn't mean he should lead. If he's bad, he's bad."

"If you were really bad, you wouldn't give a shit about the Pack under you. You're denying what you are, denying your wolf a Pack to protect because you think you will fail people you care about."

"I don't give a shit about anyone—"

"Bullshit." Daylen's eyes flashed lighter with

anger. "Bullshit, Stark. Everything is clicking into place. All the dumb shit you've done had an ulterior motive, and it's always led to protecting me, and Marsden, and now Denver. And Lyndi. You care, you just don't want anyone to know it."

"That's not true," Stark growled low. "Lyndi knows—"

"And fuck the rest of us, right?"

Daylen was getting too close to the truth and he hated it. Rage boiled through his blood, and inside of him the wolf was snarling. "Yes. Fuck you."

"I see you now, Stark. I've felt hunted for months and wondered how the hell I'm going to keep us safe, and the entire time you've been here right beside me."

"I don't give a shit if you live or die—"

"Enough!" Daylen snapped. He stood and strode to the door. "You will challenge me for Alpha, and may the best man win."

"No!" Stark roared. "You are the best man; your place isn't being challenged. You are the leader, and I kill. Those are our roles. I can be your knife, but I can't be *you*. I'll get every last member of this Pack killed. I'm not built for it."

"You called Lyndi a scaredy-cat in that vision." Daylen jammed his finger at him. "You're the scared one. You're terrified of losing people you actually care about, so you pretend we are all pieces of shit and you would piss on our carcasses if we croaked, but that's not how it really is. We aren't your mom, or your dad, or the shit Packs you belonged to before you came here. I didn't want to be Alpha either. Vager was groomed for it. The entire Pack left under Tessa's reign, and I inherited a broken throne I never wanted, but I stuck to it because no one else wanted the job. I haven't rebuilt us, I haven't added members, I haven't figured out a way to rid us of Tessa's threat." Daylen slammed his hand against his chest. "I have been the fall of this pack. I have been the Fall of Promise." He pointed at Stark. "You're the rise."

Chills rippled up Stark's spine.

And just before Daylen slammed his RV door closed, he turned and growled, "I care, too."

FIFTEEN

Denver was on the front porch with a duffel bag slung over her shoulder and a slight frown on her face.

Lyndi let the curtain fall from her fingertips and opened the door for her sister. "Hey! What are you doing here?"

Denver parted her lips to answer, but nothing came out. She tried again. "I don't know. The boys are being really weird."

"What? Come on in." As Denver passed by her, she asked, "Are you and Daylen okay?"

"I...I don't know. He asked me to come stay here for a while. Wouldn't say why. He danced around my questions. Said he and Stark are going through some stuff and need space."

"Oh my gosh," Lyndi murmured, reaching for her cell phone on the coffee table. "Stark hasn't talked to me much today, but I figured he was just really busy at work."

"When I left Daylen's, Stark's truck was still parked by his RV. He wasn't at work today."

Red flags were a-flying and alarm bells were ringing. She sent a text to Stark. *Is everything okay?*

The typing dots appeared, disappeared, and appeared again. *Miss you. I need to take care of some stuff for the next couple days. Is Denver there?*

Screw texting. Hearing his voice felt necessary right now. She connected a call to him but he didn't pick up.

Is Denver there? He texted her again.

Yes. What is happening?

Give me two days of space. Everything will be okay. I promise.

A trill of fear drifted through her. "Something big is happening."

"Yeah," Denver agreed. "Can you feel your bond at all?"

"I...I don't think I can feel it."

Denver's full lips pursed. "Daylen has slammed mine completely closed, and Marsden texted me on the way here asking why the fuck he can't feel his. He said Daylen and Stark aren't answering his calls. Said he is driving up there to figure things out and that he will message us if he has news."

"I don't like this."

Denver plopped down onto the couch and shook her head slowly, stared at the fireplace. "I don't either. Do you think Daylen is wanting to leave me?"

"Hell no. He adores you."

"He's never asked me to leave before. Maybe he's getting tired of me."

"Impossible. That boy is obsessed with you. Anyone with eyes in their head can see that when they're around you two. This feels like a Stark thing."

Denver's eyes dashed to Lyndi, and then away. "Everything has been okay between you two?"

"Well, I thought so. He gave me this." Lyndi pulled the neck of her T-shirt to the side to expose the red scar of her claiming mark.

"Oh my gosh!" Denver exclaimed, bolting for her. She ran her fingertip around the edge of it. "Stark is like the old wolves. Did yours hurt?"

"Surprisingly, no. He did it at the perfect time," she admitted, a blush heating her cheeks.

"So, it's not him leaving you. A claiming mark is from the wolf. The animal wouldn't let you go even if he tried." Denver sat back on the couch and unloaded the duffel bag from her shoulder. "Okay. Okay! Maybe it's not us."

"I think this is the part of being a Pack where we have to trust them," Lyndi said on a breath. "Maybe Alphas have to make decisions quietly that the rest of the Pack doesn't know about? I don't know."

She pulled her phone back up and texted Stark back. *Whatever is happening, I miss you too.*

That was code for the L-word for them. He would understand.

Have a couple of fun nights with Denver. If you have a pillow fight, send me pics. Also send me titty pics, and maybe one in the bathtub. Bubble bath. I'll fuck you mindless when I get back. Everything is okay. Trust me.

She read the last two words a few times to let the comfort of them slide over her panicking fox. *Trust me.* She did trust him. "They're going somewhere," she told Denver. "He said when he gets back. Maybe some kind of man-trip?"

"Gasp! Maybe he is going ring shopping for you! Maybe he's wanting Daylen to go with him and he knows if he tells me, I'll totally spill all the beans. There are no good jewelry shops around here. I know because Daylen was looking last week." She stood and made her way into the kitchen, then began opening a bottle of red wine.

Lyndi snorted. "I think the claiming mark is my ring. Sounds more likely that Daylen would be the one shopping for you."

Denver twisted around and pulled a surprised-happy face. "He has been talking about it! It makes sense on why they wouldn't tell Marsden too. He would blab to me. He's turned out to be my boy-bestie."

"Marsden?" Lyndi asked, pulling down a box of Cheez-It crackers and a pair of matching wine tumblers that both had cartoon chickens on them and the phrase 'Just a girl who likes peckers' etched into them in cursive letters. She'd bought the matching set from a garage sale for her and Denver a couple years ago, and they were their go-to wine-night glasses. "Marsden has barely said two words to me ever."

"Give it time. He is like a pack of frozen hamburger meat. He takes a long time to defrost, but is worth the wait."

Lyndi snorted and held the tumblers out for Denver to pour into them. "I think you just have the ability to open anyone up and make friends."

Denver took a sip and nodded. "Oh, that's good."

"Thanks, I got it on clearance for three dollars. Only the best stuff for my sis."

"That's probably why I like it so much." Denver took a handful of cheddar crackers from the box and took another sip of the wine, then smacked her lips. "My body rejects fancy snacks."

And from now until she stopped breathing, Lyndi would refer to anything higher caliber than Cheez-It crackers and three-dollar wine as "fancy snacks." Feeling much better, she began catching Denver up about the meeting with Stark and their parents, and settled into a surprise girls' night that she hadn't realized she needed.

Trust me.

She did trust Stark. That's how it was supposed to be. He wouldn't do anything that would hurt her, and whatever he was taking care of, she knew in her heart that he would tell her when the time was right.

And if it was indeed that Daylen was traveling into the city to shop for rings?

No one would be happier for her sister than Lyndi.

SIXTEEN

"Remember the time you kept sneaking skanky clothes to school?" Lyndi asked, flipping the page of the old yearbook.

Denver scoffed. "I don't recall that. I always wore very classy clothes. It was you who was sneaking crop tops to class."

"Girl, no. That was you! I covered for you! Mom kept asking why your backpack always looked like it was about to explode, and I told her you forgot the combination to the lock on your locker. Not that you had your whole entire ho-wardrobe in there so you could have choices when you changed in the school bathroom every morning."

"First off…" Denver grinned and took a sip of her

wine. "Thank you for covering me. My wardrobe was bomb."

Lyndi belted out a laugh. "I was a little jealous of it. I never figured out where you got the money to buy all the clothes though."

"Remember Jennifer Prague?"

Lyndi had to think hard. These were memories from a long time ago and they didn't usually talk about life this far back. "Was she the one with the braces and the glasses?"

"No, that was Stephanie Cockeral. You remember Jennifer. She came over on the weekends for like a year when I was fourteen."

"Oooooh, was she the one who always wore the shorts up her butt crack?"

"Yep! Her parents were loaded and they were going through a divorce. They were trying to win her over with letting her do whatever she wanted. And that year, she wanted to hoard all of the booty shorts and crop tops, and she was good at sharing with her bestie." Denver pointed her finger to herself.

"Well, I'm sure all the boys in your class appreciated her parents' divorce."

"Daylen didn't notice any of my awesome shirts.

He was too deep in the friendzone back then."

"And now look at him…"

"Boning me daily, even when I don't wear crop tops," Denver joked.

Lyndi tossed her head back laughing. She had a little buzz, and Denver had been hilarious all night. Though her mind constantly drifted back to Stark, she just had this feeling that he was fine, so she could cut loose and have fun with her sister.

The text notification on her phone dinged, and Lyndi perked up. Hopefully it was Stark responding to the selfie she'd sent him.

She picked her phone off the coffee table and as she read the name on that text, her heart dropped to the floor. It wasn't from Stark at all. The text had come from Jake.

She opened it and cringed as she read it. *Can we talk?*

Fuck off. For life. Send.

I'm serious. The other day shook me a little, and I've been thinking about it a lot. I'm dropping the court case. Keep your money, you're earning it. That doesn't belong to me. Can I call you?

He was dropping the case? What? "Uuuh, I have to

take a call really quick," she muttered to Denver.

"Is Stark all right?"

"It's not Stark. It's Jake."

"Ew." The look of disgust on Denver's face conjured another laugh. Lyndi was really glad she was here.

Lyndi connected a call to her deadbeat ex. When he answered, she told him, "I'm not calling to talk about anything other than the case. I'm good and happy without you. No games."

"Okay, okay. I get it, Lyn. Look, I've been talking about it with my parents and my lawyer, and I'm okay with just going our separate ways. I need you to sign the settlement though. You can take your time and read it, that's fine. I just can't drop it until all involved parties sign the paperwork to get us out of this. My lawyer already drew it up."

"Great, we can meet tomorrow at the coffee shop in town."

"Well, I was kind of hoping to get it done tonight."

He sounded too nice. Too accommodating. Too...something. "What are you doing?" she asked softly.

"Trying to get to where I can sleep easy again.

These last few months...well, they've been a lot."

"Destroying me is getting to your conscience?"

"Something like that," he muttered.

It would be nice to sign the paperwork and have something huge off her shoulders, but... "I'm hanging out with Denver tonight."

"Oh. That's okay. She can come too if you want. I'm just here with my parents. You don't have to come inside or anything. I can bring the papers outside to you when you pull up."

Lyndi narrowed her eyes at Denver. "Do you want to go with me to sign some papers?"

"If we go into town, we're stopping at the Back Door for lemon drops."

"Oh my gosh, okay. We'll be there in twenty. Can you bring the papers out to me? I don't want to see your parents."

"Sure. Lyndi?"

"Yeah?"

"I'm sorry." The line went dead.

Lyndi pulled the phone from her ear and frowned down at it as Jake's name faded from the glowing screen. In all their time together, he'd never apologized for anything. Maybe he really was changing. Perhaps the guilt was finally eating at him so much, he just wanted it all to end.

"He just said—"

"I know," Denver said, pointing to her ear. "I heard. So that was weird." Denver gave a wicked grin. "Maybe he's dying."

Lyndi giggled. Of course Denver would say that. "Wishing death on people is bad karma."

"Destroying a woman's reputation and getting her shunned from her entire community of people, all so he can get a new mate to bone, and then trying to take all the money of the woman he shamed is bad karma. I could say he should die every day for the rest of his life and I still couldn't keep up with the bad karma that needle-dick had earned."

Well, when Denver put it that way… "You have a point."

They headed out the door, and on the way out Lyndi texted Stark. *Jake is calling off the case! Heading over there to sign the paperwork. I'm relieved. It's one less thing we have to deal with. I am so ready to just move forward. I hope you are having fun, sexy-nutz.*

Smiling to herself, she sent the text and shoved the phone into her back pocket, then loaded up into

Denver's old blue clunker truck.

****

Stark knew his plan was ruined from the second Lyndi and Denver came out of the apartment and loaded up into Denver's pickup.

Fuck.

His phone vibrated in his back pocket, and he pulled it out quick, ducking behind a tree so the girls couldn't see the light from it.

Jake was the one drawing her out? Stark's mind raced. Tessa either needed them on the road or at Jake's parents' house. She didn't want to come into this territory and get ambushed. She'd always been too clever for her own good.

Oooooh he was going to enjoy killing Jake. *Fuck the rules, put me down, whatever.* That prick had allied with Tessa and was a part of this? He had to know what Tessa planned. This wasn't a fair fight. That psycho she-wolf only understood massacre. What did he have to gain? Revenge? Nah, Jake didn't care enough about his pride for that. Would Lyndi's half of the bar go to him if she was killed? That sounded about right. He would find a way. Fuckin' snake, but snakes could be dealt with. It was the she-devil Stark needed to handle first.

He dragged his gaze to Daylen, who knelt in the woods across the road from him. His Alpha's eyes had lightened to a bright gold as the truck engine roared to life. Clearly, Tessa had smelled a rat. The realization on Daylen's face said he'd figured it out too.

Daylen cast him a troubled glance and held out his hand. *Stay. Hold steady. Let them go.*

Stark's hair was down and wild because he was ready for his Change, and the breeze blew it against his cheek. The downfall to turning his mate into bait—he had to let her go. It was that or they would never flush out Tessa and her new Pack until it was too late. He needed this to end tonight, either way.

Double fuck.

He had to fight every instinct as he melted back away from the road and watched the truck zoom down the road. Lyndi and Denver were inside singing along with a song. Pretty Lyndi.

He stood to follow Daylen, who was already jogging down the hill through the woods after the girls.

Stark turned and a stabbing pain slammed into

his neck. Shit, he was snake-bit. *Wait...*

Stark pulled the syringe out of his neck, stared in confusion at the red feather at the end of it. The world sagged and melted, and Stark staggered on his feet. Blinking hard, he tried to get his vision to clear as he dragged his attention to Daylen. His alpha was yelling, running for him, pointing to something.

His voice was slowed, just a roar in his ears, and Stark tried to duck out of the way of something coming fast for his face. A tree limb?

Crack.

Stark hit the earth and his vision went dark, then partially returned. Pain, pain, pain, like lightning striking his head over and over. And as he fought to stay conscious, he saw him. Isaiah.

He knew him. Knew his face. His hair was different, but Stark recognized him. He was in Tessa's Pack when Stark had joined. Stark had fought him the first day and taken his rank.

"Remember me, motherfucker?" Isaiah murmured, his eyes bright yellow, his smile evil.

Stark couldn't talk. *Wolf, where are you?* The animal had gone silent inside of him.

"Your wolf can't help you now." Isaiah leaned in

closer. "We put him to sleep."

But something terrible was happening inside of him. Something dark and poisonous, something that was growing. Isaiah didn't understand. He hadn't figured it out.

Daylen? Where was Daylen? He couldn't see him. Couldn't sense him in the dark woods. All he could hear was a shuffling sound somewhere in the trees. He pushed the bonds open but he couldn't feel his Alpha. He couldn't feel anyone. The wolf was gagged, and his Pack was gone...Lyndi's bond was gone...and a foul, dark cloud was pulsing and growing inside of him.

Stark snarled out, "You shouldn't have done this."

SEVENTEEN

Stop!

Lyndi gasped as pain shot through her head.

Beside her, Denver slammed on the brakes and skidded them sideways to a rocking stop.

Lyndi had covered her ears at the sheer deafening volume of the word that had rocketed through her mind, but slowly removed them now. "Denver? Please tell me you heard that."

"It was Daylen's voice," she said, looking around with panic in her glowing gold eyes.

She got it. Inside of her, Lyndi's fox was clawing to get out. Daylen's voice had been filled with an order.

"He never does that," Denver whispered. "He

never gives an order like that. He sounded...he sounded..."

"Panicked."

"Yeah, and then there was pain, and then nothing. Did you feel it? The pain?"

"Head's still hurting." She scanned the dark woods that surrounded the road, but they felt off. Ominous, perhaps.

Denver gripped the steering wheel and tried to push onto the gas, but she couldn't. "Lyndi, I can't go. I can't drive." Her forearms were covered in gooseflesh.

The sight of it dredged chills up her own spine. Something felt wrong. Felt off. The woods around them were heavy and the fox inside of her felt exposed and was pushing to find a den somewhere.

"Daylen?" Denver asked in a shaking, small voice.

Lyndi jerked her attention to Denver, but she was staring at the woods illuminated by her headlights with a strange, faraway look on her face.

Confused, Lyndi searched the woods for Daylen, but he wasn't there. "No one is there," Lyndi whispered.

Denver began shaking hard. "Oh my God," she

whispered, horror written into every line of her face. Her eyes had turned black, and Lyndi waved her hand in front of her sister's face with no reaction. Her pupils were blown.

"What do you see?" Lyndi whispered.

"He's…" Tears streamed down her cheeks as she sat there frozen. "He's dead. He has to be. So much blood."

"It's not real." A wolf appeared out of the shadows, loping gracefully through the trees. A gray colored one with glowing golden eyes. Shit, shit, shit. "Denver, it's not real! Daylen isn't there!" She scrabbled to unbuckle her sister. They needed to move. That was Tessa's wolf.

Run, run, run! Her fox was chanting. *Hide, hide, hide.*

Denver shook her off and unlatched the door, kicked it open.

"No!" Lyndi screamed, pulling at Denver's arm to keep her inside.

"I have to help him!" Denver screamed, ripping out of her grasp.

"Goddammit, Denver, he's not real! It's Tessa!" Panicked, she unbuckled and jumped out the door after Denver, clipped her legs out from under her. Denver slammed onto the asphalt and Lyndi grabbed her by the waist.

Tessa was coming. Tessa was running full speed toward them and she wasn't alone! Three wolves flanked her.

Using every bit of the shifter strength she possessed, she wrestled Denver into the driver's side. No time to open the back door! Denver fought her like a banshee, and she was running out of moments left.

"Sorry," she murmured as she hauled back and blasted Denver across the face with her closed fist. Her sister's head rocked back and she went limp, and that's all she needed.

Lyndi shoved Denver's body across the bench seat and climbed in. She was blurring, going as fast as the fox empowered her to, but there was no time to shut the door before she threw the truck into drive and slammed her foot onto the gas.

The wolves were so much faster than Denver's truck. She was gunning it, but as the forward motion caught the door and brought it to a close, Tessa's snapping face appeared in between the door and the frame. Tessa latched onto Lyndi's arm and she screamed in pain as she held onto the wheel for dear life.

Jerking the wheel, she went off road and slammed into the side of a tree. With a horrible jerk, Tessa's teeth dragged through her forearm before the wolf and the door disappeared in a spray of shattering glass.

It slowed her down. Denver was muttering something incomprehensible as Lyndi got the truck to climb out of the shallow ditch and back to the road. One glance in the mirror and she knew it wasn't over. Not even close. The three wolves were trailing her, running faster and faster, and Tessa was behind them. God, she wished Tessa was dead.

Her eyes were burning with pain as she held her useless arm to her stomach and drove one handed. She had bonds, right?

"Stark!" she screamed, knowing she only had seconds left before she was going to Change. "Stark, Daylen, Marsden! Help us!"

She didn't know how to do this. Didn't know anything about Pack bonds. Could they hear her? "Stark!" Her shriek was barely audible over the roaring in her ears.

Denver was sitting up, shaking her head, arm locked on the dashboard. "What's happening?" she asked in horror as she twisted to look behind them.

"Tessa can get in your head!"

Denver looked scared as she dragged her bright-gold eyes back to her and then down to Lyndi's arm. "You're bleeding bad."

"No shit, Sherlock," she growled. She knew exactly how bad it was. The entire left side of her body had a pulse, and her eyes were freaking watering with agony. She was going to bleed out quick if she didn't Change. *Please God, let the fox help!*

"Look," Denver huffed out, pointing out the windshield.

Up ahead, there were at least a dozen wolves crowding in the middle of the road. She would've been tempted to barrel right through them if her parents weren't kneeling in the middle of the road, Jake behind them with a gun to the back of her mom's head.

There were downed trees piled up on either side of the road, so she couldn't avoid them.

Jake held up his hand and mouthed, "Stop."

Lyndi had no choice. Mom was crying, and Dad looked sick. She slammed on the brakes and skidded sideways, went up slightly on two wheels before the truck slammed back to earth and stopped.

"Change," she told Denver, because if they were going down, they were going down fighting.

Denver's face was already elongating, and in the final seconds before the red fox took her sister's skin, she could see the fury in Denver's face that Lyndi felt down to her soul.

Fuck. Jake and all of his treachery. He'd helped to kill her and her family? He'd turned traitor and helped the werewolves? Helped Tessa?

Her last act on earth would be to kill him.

"Stark, if you can hear me, I'm sorry," she whispered as her body folded in half. Fur rippled out of her skin as she fell out of the truck toward the asphalt, and as she hit the ground, she wasn't on her hands and knees. She was on all four paws.

Oh, she knew how fast she and Denver were. They couldn't fight an entire wolf pack, but they could get to Jake before he got an accurate shot off at her. Time slowed. He was lifting the gun away from her mother's head, dragging the barrel toward her, taking aim.

Coward!

She leapt through the air, hating the slow-motion smile on Jake's evil face as he pulled his finger back on the trigger.

Denver was too fast for that motherfucker though. Dumb fuck had focused too much on Lyndi and not enough on the red blur that slammed into his legs, jerking him to the side as he went airborne. The discharge of the weapon was deafening this close, and she could feel the wind from the bullet as it went just a little too high above her head.

She landed on Jake's shoulder as he hit the road and latched her teeth onto his throat. She had to be fast because the wolves were on the move. Lyndi wanted her last act on this earth to be vengeance— for her, for Denver, for her parents...for Stark because he was about to lose her, and it wasn't fair. They had both been safe with each other...they'd finally been safe.

Lyndi clamped her sharp teeth onto his throat and with every ounce of hatred she possessed, she ripped it out. The first gurgle of his impending death echoed through the woods as one of the wolves clamped his jaws around her back.

Lyndi went sailing through the air and landed on her feet, sliding to the very edge of the concrete road. Her bad leg gave and she went down, rolling into the shallow ditch. Denver was fighting a wolf savagely and a black wolf was leaping through the air toward Lyndi.

This was the end.

Stark, I'm sorry, I'm sorry, I'm sorry.

She curled her lips back, flattened her ears, and swore she would do as much damage as she could on her way out.

Just as the wolf's paws landed on either side of her and his razor-sharp teeth stretched for her, something huge barreled into the side of him, and the animal disappeared.

A power-filled black fog rolled across her vision. In the seconds it took to clear, the black wolf was on its side, staring blankly at her, his eyes devoid of life.

A roar that was half howl, half monster shook the woods. The ground beneath her shook so hard, she flattened down to her belly and backed up a few steps, closer to the shadows of the woods.

On the road, illuminated by the headlights of

Denver's crippled car, a war was raging, but it wasn't just Denver fighting anymore. Three wolves had joined in and they were shredding everyone. Daylen? Marsden? But who was the other? That wasn't Stark. Were Tessa's wolves turning on her? Daylen was raging with Tessa, fighting to kill, and Denver was engaged with a white wolf with hate-filled silver eyes.

Her parents were running off the road. Why weren't they Changing? Dad was shielding Mom with his body, and there was a wolf running for them. Not a fair fight. Lyndi bolted for them and cut the wolf off just as it reached them. She sank her teeth into the nape of his neck, holding on as tightly as she could, but he threw her easily. Stupid werewolves were so strong. She spun and grabbed onto the back of his leg to give her parents a few moments. *Change!* Why the hell weren't they Changing?

The wolf turned on her and those impossibly strong jaws latched onto her body. Lyndi closed her eyes and waited for the pain, but the wolf yelped and fell to the ground. Lyndi went down with him, and stunned, she shook her way out of the dead wolf's jaws. Above her stood a monster. The creature stood to his full height. He walked like a human, but he was covered in charcoal gray fur. He was two times the size of a normal man, and he had the face of a wolf. But those eyes. The terror drifted from her in an instant. Those eyes belonged to Stark.

Tonight, Stark wasn't a wolf. He was a monster.

"They can't Change," he growled in a voice of nightmares. He gestured to her parents, who were huddling near the tree-line, under the low-hanging branches of a giant pine. "Keep them safe."

Yes.

She thought it, but she couldn't feel the bond to him at all.

"Denver," he barked. "Here."

Denver fell to the ground from her fight and bolted for Lyndi like she couldn't control her body. She was snarling, and her face was covered in red. Was that what Lyndi looked like, too?

Stark, the half-Changed wolf, strode out onto the road and turned into a weapon. That's all she could think of. He was smooth and lethal. There was no hesitation as he worked his way through Tessa's entire pack. Two wolves tried to run from him but he dropped to all fours and stopped them in two strides.

Lyndi couldn't keep her eyes off him. Never in her

life had she witnessed a war like this. A wolf leapt onto his back, but Stark spun easily, grabbed it by the neck, and chucked it right into the jaws of a charging bear. A bear. There was a bear.

"Oh my God. That's Divar," Denver whispered.

Lyndi cast a quick glance back and saw that Denver was Changed into her human form, crouched on the ground, covered in blood and claw marks, her gold eyes full of awe.

"Daylen called in reinforcements." Denver looked up into the sky, and Lyndi followed her gaze just in time to see a Murder of crows fly across the break in the canopy.

An inhuman roar rattled the night and shook the ground beneath her. Stark stood up from the last battle, and as he met Lyndi's eyes, he dropped Tessa's limp wolf onto the road with the rest of her poisonous army.

"We should go," Denver murmured in a faraway voice.

Wh-what? Lyndi wondered numbly. They couldn't leave. The Pack was here. Stark was here.

Denver was tugging at her hind leg. "Lyndi, we should really go," she said louder.

A mountainous shadow covered the road and the powerful wind that followed flattened all of them but Stark, who tracked the movement with his ice-cold blue eyes.

Denver yelled, "They have a dragon!"

The bear was already running, and the extra wolf too. Daylen and Marsden bolted toward Denver. Stark was running straight for Lyndi with long, powerful strides. "Through there!" he bellowed, pointing to the woods behind her.

Ahead of them, Lyndi's parents were already running beside Denver, and Stark followed with Lyndi. Her front leg wasn't working from where Tessa had ripped it. It wasn't working at all! She pitched forward and Stark's massive hand stretched out and snatched her right out of the fall. He didn't even miss a step, just pushed even faster with her tucked under his arm. Behind them, the road lit up with a long, scorching stream of fire. Hot air blasted against her, and she yelped with the blistering heat that lashed against her.

"Faster!" he yelled. But with a grunt of agony, he fell forward and his wolf ripped out of him the rest of the way. Lyndi went tumbling end over end. Stark's massive wolf ran a few yards as she limped after him, and he circled back, then bolted, circled back. *Come on!* He seemed to say.

Another blast of fire leveled the woods behind them, closer this time, and the heat was excruciating. It was unending.

Stark jumped for her, covered her body completely with his, and his body tensed as he endured the heat for both of them.

Smoke filled the woods, choking her and burning her eyes. The ground was hot where she tried to step out from under the protection Stark provided. She and Stark looked up at a whooshing noise and she could see him—the dragon. He was the size of a mountain with black scales and tattered gargoyle wings. And when he beat those wings above them, the wind he created laid them all flat on the ground. The air was sucked out of her lungs, and terror surged through her.

Denver stood there, her gaze trailing where the dragon had disappeared over the trees. "That's Nuke."

"There's dragons," her mom murmured in shock.

"Why was he here?" her dad asked.

"For cleanup." Denver looked at their parents. "There won't be a trace of Tessa's Pack left."

Daylen's black wolf was stalking this way. Lyndi perked her ears up and growled.

"Daylen?" Denver asked, confusion infusing her tone.

Stark huffed a sigh and stood, led Daylen away from Lyndi. What was happening?

Marsden's gray wolf trotted toward them through the trees, yipping, and the air was charged with a tension Lyndi didn't understand. Between the smoke and dominance, it was hard to breathe. The two wolves sauntered away, their tails low, ears back, and snarls in their throats as they walked side by side deeper into the black smog.

Daylen moved first, leaning into Stark as he snapped his teeth, missing by inches because Stark had been ready. *No!*

Lyndi bolted for them, but Marsden's wolf cut her off. He flattened his ears and growled at her, shook his head slowly.

But they're friends! They're in the same Pack!

There had already been too much war, too much violence, and now this? Friends fighting friends? It was too much! She yipped a pleading cry as they drew blood.

Both wolves were already shredded, coats matted with wet, dark patches and slashes. Their muzzles were covered in blood, and Daylen's ear had a huge notch taken out of it. The fighting was brutal. It was a blur of battle, and the sound of their snarling echoed through the woods. It was spinning and biting and snapping and bleeding, and then it was done. Just as fast as it had started, it ended with Daylen on his back and Stark's teeth around his throat.

"No!" Denver screamed. The word echoed through the mountains, but neither of the wolves moved.

Whatever their wolves said to each other, Lyndi would never quite understand. There was this charged moment of power as the two clashing titans glared at each other. As Daylen's throat was at Stark's mercy.

Stark clamped down, and Denver gasped, took a step forward.

Stark's bright-blue eyes cast to Denver, and he released her mate. A few steps back and he wanted for Daylen to stand.

The Alpha clambered up on all fours and, blood dripping down his chin, he perked his ears up and his eyes softened. Slowly, Daylen cocked his head to the side and exposed his throat.

Alpha. The word whispered through Lyndi's head, and she gasped. She could feel them again. Could feel Daylen and Denver now, their bonds. She could feel Marsden. She could feel Stark most of all. Right now, he felt...resigned. Defeated, almost, but he hadn't been defeated. He'd won a fight with Daylen. With the Alpha. No...the former Alpha.

It was staring to hit her as Marsden lowered to his belly, flattened his ears back, and canted his head to the side to show his throat to Stark. Denver dropped to her knees beside Daylen, rested her hand on his back, her gold eyes gone wide. She tilted her head.

This was the moment Lyndi would never forget for the rest of her life. She'd asked to be part of this Pack, and in some ways she was, but Daylen had denied her before. Now? In the haze of smoke, bodies wrecked by war, her friends had bowed one by one before her mate.

Stark studied the ground before him, and then

dragged his bright-blue eyes to her, and she could see the question there.

Will you?

Lyndi had never been so proud of a man. She'd been dragged through every emotion, but to end on this one? Pride? Love?

Yes. Lyndi limped forward on her three good legs and lowered to her belly. If she could cry with happiness in this body, she would've.

She tilted her head, and Stark lowered his massive head to hers. He pressed his nose against her neck, and exhaled a relieved sound. Inside of her, she could feel Stark's relief.

Tessa had brought hell to their quiet little town, but they were still standing.

Her family was safe, her mate was safe.

Her Pack was safe.

She wasn't a cull fox, and Stark wasn't a cull wolf. They'd just had to find their place, together.

A keening sound escaped her throat, and Stark threw his head back and let off a howl. Daylen joined them, and Marsden. Denver was crying, and wiped her eyes before she threw her head back and gave a human howl.

Her mom stood to the side, squeezed tightly to her dad's side. She was crying, but she was smiling. Could see feel this? Could they feel how happy she and Denver were?

Everything was okay.

Everything was always going to be okay; they'd just needed to fight a little to get here. They'd had to fight for the lives they wanted.

From this day forward, Lyndi would never been shunned again. There was certainty in that.

And neither would her Alpha, her mate...her Stark.

EPILOGUE

Stark was still here.

His skin bore a whole new set of scars, but his mate didn't mind them. He'd earned them protecting her, and if he had it all to do over again, he would do the same. Always.

It had been two months since the war, and they still hadn't added more wolves to their numbers. They would at some point, but right now, there was no threat. Tessa and her Pack were all dead and in the belly of the dragon, and the Promise Falls Pack had scratched and clawed for a stretch of peace.

Someday they would expand. Lord knew they'd received offers and applications for new members after the devastation they'd caused to an entire Pack under the powerful and volatile Tessa Hoda, but Stark had decided to build their existing bonds before they added more.

Power attracted wolves, and this Pack had established that they were hard to kill.

Tonight would be an easy night. A good-for-the-soul night. A bonfire night with Daylen, Marsden, Denver, and especially Lyndi. Denver had called a Pack party, and he thought he knew exactly why. He would bet just about everything he loved that Denver was carrying Daylen's pup. Stark wasn't destined to be a dad, but he was determined to be a good uncle. And it would do Lyndi good to have a baby around. She would've made an incredible mom, but their story wasn't over. The wolf who had tried to raise him hadn't been able to have her own children, but Vanna had paid attention to the pups in the Pack, and she'd become important to Stark, even back then when he didn't know how to love.

Vanna.

He'd been sitting here staring at the old, tattered gray backpack in the corner of his closet for ten minutes.

The RV door opened and Lyndi called out,

"Stark?"

"In here," he called.

She padded down the hallway and came to stand beside him. She slipped her hand into the crook of his elbow and the wolf inside of him settled in an instant. He brushed his fingertips down the long scars across her forearm. He was so damn proud that she was his mate.

"Is that the backpack?" she asked.

Stark leaned over and kissed the top of her head as an answer. "I have a present for you."

"You give me presents all the time. How will I ever pay you back?" she asked.

Her voice was high and excited, and he looked down at her to see her eyes had lightened to gold. Nervous, excited energy radiated from her. "Are you okay?" he asked.

Her grin was the most beautiful thing he'd ever seen. "I'm more than okay. I'm so happy."

She must've figured out Denver was wanting to make a special announcement. Good, sweet mate. She wasn't jealous or pitying herself for Denver starting the family she couldn't have. She was happy for her sister. Selfless woman. God, he loved every single thing about her.

"Everyone is waiting for you," she whispered. "Daylen brought a whole cooler of your favorite beers."

Daylen had turned out to be his best friend. His first best friend. Oh, they still fought like hell most of the time, but he seemed to understand Stark more and more, and there was unimaginable value in that. Stark leaned forward and pulled the backpack out, then set it on the bed and unzipped the single zipper.

Inside, there were only three things—the little toy cowboy he'd kept from his youth, the old photograph of his mother, and the folded piece of paper with Vanna's number on it.

He sat on the edge of the bed and pulled the little cowboy out. He studied the worn paint job for a few moments before he offered it to Lyndi. Pretty girl, she placed her hand over her mouth and teared up as she took it from his hand.

"For me?"

He nodded, and hoped to God she understood what he meant by it. Lyndi placed herself between his legs and hugged him tight, cupping his head against her chest and resting her cheek against the top of his hair. "I love you too," she whispered.

Clever little fox.

She placed a gentle kiss on top of his head, then cupped his face and dragged his gaze up to hers. "You should call her now. You should tell her you're worth a damn."

She remembered. He hadn't been ready to make that call, because he wanted to feel like his life was together completely. He wanted to make her proud.

Lyndi gave him an emotional smile. "Call her."

And then she made her way out of the RV and left him there staring at the folded piece of paper.

He was ready. Stark plucked the paper out of the bottom of his backpack and unfolded it, pulled his phone out of his back pocket, and dialed the number before he could change his mind.

On the first ring, a phone sounded outside. His ears perked up and he turned his head. With each ring, it matched a ring outside.

No one answered.

He retyped the number, just in case he'd dialed it wrong. And as the ringing began again, the ringing matched outside. What the hell?

Stark strode through his RV and pushed open the

door, the phone still pressed to his ear.

Outside, the others were sitting in plastic lawn chairs around the bonfire, and Marsden was staring down at his ringing phone, clasped in his hands. His eyes held ghosts as he lifted his phone to show Stark the screen. The caller ID said Stark's name.

Confused, Stark stepped down the stairs and onto solid ground as he hung up the phone. "That's Vanna's number."

Marsden nodded, and ran his hand through his short, dark hair. "I've been waiting for you to call that number for a long time."

"I don't..." Stark looked around at the matching bafflement on the others' faces, including Lyndi, who came to stand beside him. "I don't understand."

"Vanna passed away," Marsden said. "She was my..." He swallowed hard. "Well, she took me in from a bad situation, and I grew up hearing stories about a wild little wolf-boy that slipped through the cracks. A boy she wasn't able to save. A boy she thought about a lot. When she passed, she had me take over her number, just in case you ever got to where you were supposed to go and gave her a call. She wanted someone to hear you'd made it, even if she couldn't."

Marsden sniffed and shrugged his shoulders. "So, I left my Pack, and I went to track down a wolf-boy who had turned into a monster, heading for a last chance Pack, and I watched you spinning out, and hating everyone, and most of all hating yourself. And when everything fell apart, and all those wolves left the Pack, I was angry. Pissed. You were getting worse and I started to think you would never call Vanna's number. Like you would never feel like you were okay. I wanted you to be okay because it felt like Vanna could rest easy, and she was an angel. She deserves to rest." His lip trembled, and he ducked his gaze. "I have something for you. Vanna told me to only give it to you if you called that number."

He stood and made his way to his truck, opened the passenger side door, and pulled an envelope from the glove compartment. It was wrinkled and one of the corners had been ripped. Marsden hesitated, and then handed it to Stark.

Stark cast a glance at Daylen, who looked completely rocked. "Holy shit," he murmured.

Stark had no words as he opened that envelope with shaking fingers. He pulled out the single, yellow, ruled notebook paper and unfolded it.

Dear Stark Devlin Wulfson...

He could hear the words in Vanna's voice, and then he couldn't. His eyes were acting funny. They were all hot and blurry. He shook his head, trying to clear the confounding sensation that had taken over his face. A drop of water splatted onto his cursive-written name, and he shook his head again. What was happening to him?

"Do you want me to read it for you?" Lyndi whispered beside him.

Unable to answer, Stark nodded and handed it to her. He sat in the chair beside her and stared at the fire as she began to read.

"Dear Stark Devlin Wulfson. I feel like I'm the only one left in the world who knows your whole name, but I hope I'm wrong. If you're reading this, it means a couple things. One, I'm gone. If that's the case, know that I tried to hang on. I prayed for your call every day, and you should know I never lost hope. There was good in you, boy, you were just too bogged down in the tragedies of your life to see it. I saw it though.

Two, you're reading this if you made something

of yourself. It means you called the number I gave to you. Marsden will have it if I'm not around. I've already talked to him about it. Call me a hopeful old woman, but I always imagined a life for you. I hope you've trained your wolf to be the Alpha he was born to be. Anyone could've seen your potential if they'd just paid attention. If you have ended up where I pray you ended up, it means you found your potential by yourself, with no one telling you what you could be, and there is great power in that. It means you learned yourself. It means you're alive, and that's pretty damn important to me.

I have regrets. I wish I would've known how to defy that old Alpha's orders, and defy my mate, and drag you into my home and keep you. I wish I didn't feel so helpless back then. I never did have pups of my own, but know you were thought about as one. You had a momma-wolf out there worrying over your soul. I hope you found a mate who reminds you of your purpose, and pushes you to be better. I hope you push her to be better, too.

I wish I could've heard your voice telling me you made it, but I'll settle with you reading this letter. Somewhere out there, I'm smiling from ear to ear that you're reading this.

You were always cared about.

Keep going.

Vanna"

A sob escaped Lyndi as she read the last word, and she melted into his lap. She wiped his cheeks, and her fingertips came back wet. "And you're an Alpha now," Lyndi whispered thickly.

It was Marsden who spoke next. His words came out deep and emotional. "Vanna would've been so fuckin' proud of you, man."

How had Marsden kept this secret for so long? His entire purpose for being in this Pack, and for sticking around all these years, was because of Stark? Because of Vanna?

His mind was completely overcome with emotion right now, and he hugged her tightly, resting his cheek against hers as he nodded a thank you to Marsden.

"Stark," Lyndi whispered, sniffling.

"Yeah?"

She slid out of his lap and went straight to her knees in the dirt between his legs. Her eyes were full of tears, and her cheeks were the most beautiful shade of pink from crying. "I have something to tell you."

All intelligent thought had left the territory, so dumbly he murmured, "Okay."

"There is going to be a pup."

He grinned emotionally up at Denver. "I knew it."

Denver shook her head, and wore the strangest smile.

"No," Lyndi murmured softly. "I mean there is going to be a pup for us."

Stark frowned. "We are adopting?"

"No." Lyndi inhaled deeply. "Jake was wrong."

Warmth dumped into his chest cavity as realization hit him. Stark jerked up straight and leaned forward. "What are you saying?" He couldn't stop the hope that consumed his voice if he tried.

"I'm going to have a baby. Your baby."

He stood and lifted her in one movement. She wrapped her legs around him and was just...sobbing. Overwhelmed, he didn't even know what he was saying. Just nonsensical things that tumbled out of his mouth. "Are you serious? You're serious. Oh my God, oh my God, oh my God. Lyndi, oh my God."

Denver was crying before she even embraced

them, and Stark threw his free arm around her. Daylen wrapped them up next and that damn burning in his eyes was back.

He was going to be a dad. An Alpha and a dad, and he was able to give Lyndi the life she wanted? The family?

"I'm going to be better." He didn't know how to say better than his dad because none of them would understand but Lyndi. "I'm going to be better," he repeated mindlessly.

Marsden stood and hesitated on the outside of the circle, canted his head. And just before he wrapped them up in a hug, he said, "You're going to do just fine."

And he didn't know why, but damn, it sounded like Marsden's words belonged to Vanna too, and this moment was everything.

This wasn't his last chance Pack anymore...

This was his beginning.

THE RISE OF PROMISE

Other Books in The Wolves of Promise Falls Series

The Fall of Promise (Book 1)

The Blood of Promise (Book 3)

About the Author

T.S. Joyce is devoted to bringing hot shifter romances to readers. Hungry alpha males are her calling card, and the wilder the men, the more she'll make them pour their hearts out. She lives in the PNW with a mysterious giant hunkyman, a make-shift family, a herd of awesome kiddos, plenty of farm animals, and devotes her life to writing big stories. Foodie, bear whisperer, chicken-momma, thief of tiny bottles of awesome smelling hotel shampoo, nap connoisseur, romantic comedy fanatic, and bite-sized cattle rancher.

Bear Shifters? She's got 'em.

Smoldering Alpha Hotness? Yup yup!

Sexy Scenes? Fasten up your girdles, ladies and gents, it's gonna to be a wild ride.

For more information on T. S. Joyce's work,
visit her website at
www.tsjoyce.com

Printed in Great Britain
by Amazon

15947456R00140